I0729877

SIDE EFFECTS MAY INCLUDE DANCING

BY JAX FREY

Side Effects May Include Dancing

Printed in the United States of America
First Printing 2025
ISBN # paperback: 978-1-7331582-5-1
Cover Illustration: *Side Effects May Include Dancing* by Jax Frey

Side Effects May Include Dancing
Acrylic on Canvas
Artwork by Jax Frey

SONG AND DANCE

By Mary Beth Magee
Mississippi Poetry Society 2025 Poet of the Year
Author of The (LOL)4 Mysteries,

Inspired by "Life Music" painting by Jax Frey

The song starts with a single note,
One finger, on one key.
Resonance stretches from the piano string
To the heartstrings,
Gaining strength by the moment.
Vibrations lead to movement,
First a toe tap, then a shoulder twitch,
A hip sway and a head nod.
A second note sounds, then a third, and more.
The song builds,
And with it, the dance grows
To a crescendo of celebration,
The music of life,
Which is lifeblood to us all.

*This book is dedicated to the Seekers—
those who question, listen, stumble, rise, and keep going.
This is for you.*

ON ENLIGHTENMENT

"You are here for no other purpose than to realize your inner divinity and manifest your inner enlightenment. Foster peace in your own life and then apply the Art to all that you encounter."

—Morihei Ueshiba

"Your own Self-Realization is the greatest service you can render the world."

—Ramana Maharshi

"…the past gives you an identity and the future holds the promise of salvation, of fulfillment in whatever form. Both are illusions."

—Eckhart Tolle

"You are never alone. You are eternally connected with everyone."

—Amit Ray

"According to Vedanta, there are only two symptoms of enlightenment, just two indications that a transformation is taking place within you toward a higher consciousness. The first symptom is that you stop worrying. Things don't bother you anymore. You become light-hearted and full of joy. The second symptom is that you encounter more and more meaningful coincidences in your life, more and more synchronicities. And this accelerates to the point where you actually experience the miraculous."

—Deepak Chopra

"There is a candle in your heart, ready to be kindled.
There is a void in your soul, ready to be filled.
You feel it, don't you?"

—Rumi

"In the blink of an eye, everything can change. So, forgive often and love with all your heart."

—Zig Ziglar

CAST OF CHARACTERS

Bertie Ryan: Owner of The Bump and Grind Coffeehouse.
The Bookies:
- **Della Davis:** Bertie's best friend.
- **Bonnie**
- **Sue**
- **Cathy**

Maddie Maloney: Bertie's Aunt
Shirley Bird: Maddie's neighbor
Sharon Brown: Maddie's friend
Michael Gray: Maddie's Attorney
Gladys Yurt: Maddie's childhood friend
Synthra Lewis: CEO of Neurosea, Inc.
Lindy Mailer: Synthra's assistant
Susan Skoog: Reporter for WBRV TV
Buddy Bushey: Governor of Louisiana
Glen Lacombe: Mayor of New Orleans
Bob Gleason: Health Inspector

PROLOGUE

Synthra Lewis, the obsessively thin forty-year-old CEO of Neurosea, Inc., stood at the head of her Board of Directors in the Dallas conference room. Her red-soled heels clicked with authority, complementing her tailored, navy blue power suit, pale skin, and sleek bob. Behind her sat her young, new assistant, Lindy Mailer—competent, quiet, and always ready to jump in and help her boss. This morning, Lindy wore one of the two pairs of brown polyester pants she owned with a white blouse and her forever-present ponytail while handling the digital presentation flashing on the large screen behind them.

"As you can see," Synthra said, gesturing toward a bar chart on the screen, "Sales of *Mirajubil,* our top antidepressant, continue to climb dramatically every month. There seems to be no end to public demand for the product."

Board member, Mike Arnold, leaned forward, "To what do you attribute this increase in sales, Synthra?"

She smiled. "We're living in some pretty trippy times, Mike— politically, environmentally, financially, you name it. The world is a pressure cooker, and anxiety is at an all-time high. Mental health is no longer the taboo topic it once was. Everyone *talks* about therapy, but more people want a quick fix. And that's where we come in. Add to that the best marketing team in the industry—every time we air one of our commercials, someone's calling their doctor asking for *Mirajubil.*"

Synthra clicked her pen for emphasis and let her gaze sweep the room. "Bottom line: *Mirajubil* is a runaway hit."

The meeting wrapped up with handshakes and congratulations. When the room finally emptied, Lindy hesitated, then blurted out the question to her boss that had been gnawing at her since she joined the company.

"Synthra, do you ever wonder if we're going too far? I know that antidepressants help a lot of people, but our numbers are astronomical. Doesn't it ever seem that we might be doing more harm than good? I mean, those drugs can have so many side effects."

Synthra froze mid-motion and fixed Lindy with a frosty stare. Then slowly, she clicked her pen again.

"Lindy, how long have you worked here now?"

"Three months," Lindy said quietly. She instantly regretted her question. Synthra was notorious for going through assistants faster than paper towels. Lindy, a young, single mom, needed this job. Her honesty often got the better of her, and now she feared she'd gone too far.

Synthra studied her for a beat longer, then nodded, as if deciding something.

"Just remember, Lindy. We're helping people. Most folks are struggling these days, and we give them what they need." Synthra continued, "And honestly? If it was up to me, everyone would be on *Mirajubil*." Mentally, she added, "*Everyone and their children, too.*"

She smiled toothily at Lindy, then strode from the room.

Lindy exhaled. She felt part horror, part relief. She hadn't been fired, thank goodness, but the message was clear. Along with the other hundreds of Neurosea employees who needed their jobs, she now knew that at Neurosea, personal ethics were best left at the door.

CHAPTER 1

ertie Ryan's eyes shifted nervously as she barreled down I-55 from New Orleans towards Natchez, Mississippi. The sixty-year-old owner of the Bump and Grind Coffeehouse in New Orleans smoothed out her long, flowing purple skirt and resettled her low-hanging amethyst pendant. Her blouse was loose and berry, her favorite color, because it brought out her high color, her long salt and pepper hair, and bright blue eyes. She felt pretty today, but it did not stop the low hum of anxiety that had settled in her chest like an uninvited houseguest. It had been that way for weeks now. Maybe months. She couldn't be sure anymore.

The daily news—relentless, divisive, chaotic—had a way of creeping into her bones, even when she tried to ignore it. Where she once rolled her eyes and turned the volume down on her TV, now she found herself stewing over headlines, unable to shake the sense that the world was teetering off its axis. Even small things—an angry driver, a neighbor's political yard sign, a tense conversation on the TV—seemed to hit her harder than they should.

She had even considered making an appointment with her doctor. Not for anything physical, exactly, but to ask if she should be worried. Was this normal? Was everyone this tightly wound lately? She wasn't sure if she needed a prescription or a silent retreat. Probably both.

Today, she had more reason than usual to be anxious and upset, as she was on a dreaded personal mission. Her favorite ninety-year-old Aunt, Maddie Maloney, had died the week before. Bertie was on her way to the service. She didn't expect it to be very well attended. Aunt Maddie was reclusive, peculiar, and sometimes not very nice, but that only added to Bertie's great affection for her. Her aunt's unique sense of humor tickled Bertie's funny bone. Maddie Maloney had lived in a beautiful old, white wedding-cake of a house in Natchez. Its two stories housed her two cats and several thousand books. At Maddie's age, she'd had few friends left, and Bertie often felt neglectful. She wished she could visit more, but it was impossible, what with taking care of the Bump and Grind every day. But the two of them had spoken on the phone often, Bertie on her iPhone and Maddie on her old yellow Bakelite kitchen phone, still attached to the wall.

It was Maddie's neighbor, Shirley Bird, who had checked in on Maddie occasionally over the years, and, thank God, had adopted the two cats since Maddie's death. Her aunt had passed away in her bed on a June morning from natural causes. It was Shirley who notified Bertie of her passing, and it was her Aunt's attorney, Michael Gray, who sent Bertie the details of the small service to be held at her aunt's house. Her aunt had requested cremation and for her neighbor to spread her ashes in the backyard underneath the rose bushes. Mr. Gray also mentioned something that took Bertie by surprise. Aunt Maddie had included Bertie in her will. It had never occurred to Bertie that her aunt would leave anything to her, but now that she was thinking about it, she thought, "*Well, I guess that makes sense. I am her only living relative.*"

As her thoughts expanded, Bertie became horrified. She was at a point in her life where she was comfortable. She had a good-boned old house in the Carrollton section of New Orleans, and she also owned the Bump and Grind Coffeehouse just a few blocks away, which was an established and favorite hangout for the neighborhood. So, she wasn't particularly in monetary need at the moment. Still, mixed in with her grief over losing her aunt, Bertie couldn't help but wonder what her inheritance might be.

"Oh, dear Lord! What if she left me the house?" she thought, and had to pull her lead foot off the accelerator. She had a habit of going a speed to match her heartbeat—and in this case, it was racing. The idea of such a huge inheritance almost made her pull over with mental exhaustion. There was a lifetime of possessions and books crammed into the huge, old place. She almost felt like turning the car around and going to bed for a week.

She felt guilty thinking of these things when all she wanted to do was remember good times with her aunt, with whom she had spent many a weekend visiting as a child and even as a teenager. Aunt Maddie would invite her up to Natchez often, all by herself. Bertie's mom would drive her up on a Friday afternoon and pick her up on Sunday. Then the two of them would take Maddie's golf cart all over town. Her aunt even let her drive sometimes, even though it wasn't exactly legal. But that's one of the things Bertie loved about her aunt. She was unapologetic, unpredictable, and always laughing. The two of them had a ball together.

Her push and pull of emotions continued until she drove into Natchez and pulled in front of the big house. Bertie hurried up the long walkway and the front porch steps. The wrap-around old Southern porch was complete with lush Boston ferns and white rocking chairs. She would have liked to stop and admire the old live oak in the yard and the gorgeous, blue hydrangeas blooming next to the steps, but the service would be starting at any moment.

She gave a quick knock, then opened the old, heavy front door and let herself inside. She headed straight to the parlor where only three people were waiting to start the service.

"Small service is right," thought Bertie grimly.

There was Shirley Bird, her aunt's neighbor, a round little woman with gray hair wearing a Jackie Kennedy-style pillbox hat. Also present was Sharon Brown, a local Natchez cafe owner with flowing red hair over a bright green dress and bright red lipstick that matched her heels. And finally, there was Attorney Michael Gray, a tall, dapper, older gentleman with a kindly face and a penchant for tweed. All three were sitting in the living room around a coffee table which held a cremation urn in the center. Maddie hadn't requested clergy, as she had her own ideas about the deity.

After introductions were made, Mr. Gray quietly asked everyone to stay after the service so they could conclude Maddie's legal business as well.

It wasn't much of a service. They each went around their small circle and said their piece about Maddie.

Shirley, the neighbor, went first. "As you know, Maddie kept to herself, but we looked out for each other. In recent years, it was hard to keep up with some of her peculiar antics, like the time I caught her out in her yard, gardening in her beloved roses—stark naked. I called out 'good morning' to her, and she shouted something back to me and waved like it was the most natural thing in the world, then took off like a jackrabbit back into her house." She shook her head at the memory.

Bertie choked back a surprised chuckle. She knew her aunt to be a character as far back as she could remember. She was Bertie's dad's sister, and whenever someone in the family mentioned Aunt Maddie back then, her dad invariably threw an eyeroll into the conversation. Still, he adored his sister, and so did Bertie.

Shirley went on, "For some reason, Maddie got a little nuttier towards the end. Maybe it was a touch of dementia, who knows. But I have to give her this much—she had the most extraordinary roses I've ever seen. You can see for yourself in the backyard. Huge things, with colors that are out of this world. I used to think that maybe gardening in the buff just might be the secret to her rose success. I never had the nerve to try it. I mean, that's all I would need—to be carted off by the local police at my age. Still…" Her voice grew wistful, clearly with garden envy, and then she suddenly sat down in an abrupt finish.

Sharon Brown, the Natchez cafe owner, glanced around and then struggled to her feet in her tightly belted green dress and said loudly,

"Maddie Maloney was the orneriest woman I ever met." She nodded at the others, daring them to disagree, and they didn't. Sharon was obviously a woman who was used to dominating a room. She spoke abruptly, but her heart of gold showed through her words. "I often brought meals to her here at the house. She'd call the cafe, order a roasted veggie sandwich each and every time, breakfast or lunch, and then demand that I deliver it within twenty minutes. As if I had time to drop everything and make house calls. Still, I liked the old coot. She was bossy and knew what she wanted. Always reminded me of—well, me." She plopped back down in her chair and immediately checked her phone for texts from the cafe. Satisfied, she looked around and said, "Who's next? Let's wrap this up."

Bertie got to her feet, thinking about Maddie. She hadn't really expected to say anything at the service, but she did feel as though she should honor her aunt. As peculiar as she had been with others, she had been especially kind to Bertie. She started with, "First off, I want to thank y'all for your kindness to my aunt. I can tell that y'all meant something special to her…" Sharon gave a little snort. Bertie went on, "Seriously. Aunt Maddie, as you said, was certainly her own woman. But after my mom died, I had no other family except her. And she had me. We talked every week or so, and I have to say that Aunt Maddie had the best laugh I've ever heard. It brought me great joy to try to get a chuckle out of her when we talked. And she was always willing to listen. And, well, I loved her."

Bertie glanced towards the cremation urn on the coffee table. "You'll be missed, Aunt Maddie." She felt tears starting to puddle in her hazel eyes, so she sat down and fished for a tissue in her bag.

Last to stand was Attorney Michael Gray. "Let me say first that I'm very sorry for your loss, Ms. Ryan. I've been Maddie Maloney's attorney and friend for over twenty-five years. While not the easiest client, she was one of my favorites. I never knew what she would do next, and I grew to like that about her. She took me to task over the years taking care of her business, but, like you say, Ms. Ryan, she had a great laugh." He smiled a bit in remembrance and went on, "And Maddie didn't stop being unpredictable with her passing. As you know, she had me make a will for her. After this ceremony, I'll go over the details of that document, seeing as how Ms. Ryan is from out of town and only in for the day. So now, if no one has anything more to say, we should take care of Maddie's ashes as she requested."

The others nodded and stood while Shirley picked up the urn. All four solemnly traipsed out the back door and into Maddie's rose garden. A walkway looped around the garden, and the roses surrounded a large concrete sundial. Everyone but Bertie had seen Maddie's roses lately, but they were still awestruck at the sight. Bertie, herself, was nothing short of gobsmacked. She stopped in her tracks and stared. She expected the roses to be pretty, but the backyard was filled with rose bushes of all sizes and shapes. Each was healthy with bright green leaves reaching towards the heavens. But the roses themselves were the clear stars of the show. There were blooms of every color one could imagine. Some were nearly a foot across. Bertie's mouth fell open as she reached out a hand to caress one of the huge flowers.

"How in the world?" she breathed.

Shirley whispered seriously, "I told you! I think the naked dancing did this!"

Bertie wandered down the rows of rosebushes and found to her amazement that one bush grew roses that were actually almot square. Another was tall and had iridescent orange blooms. And if that weren't enough, yet another had alternate black and white petals.

"What the heck, Aunt Maddie? I can't believe this!" thought Bertie.

Sharon Brown interrupted Bertie's reverie and tapped her watch pointedly. "We need to get on with it, Bertie. I don't mean any disrespect, but I've got a cafe full of customers right about now."

Shirley took the hint and wrestled with the top of the cremation urn. She finally got it off, and, leaning over to the base of the nearest rosebush, she said, "Goodbye, old neighbor. Go with God, Maddie. I hope you're dancing naked in heaven's roses."

She sprinkled ashes under several bushes and then held the urn upside down, tapping it to work out the last of it.

After a moment, Attorney Gray said softly, "Well, I'll head back to the house now and wait for everyone to finish up out here. Then we'll get to the will. He turned and proceeded up the garden path towards the house.

Shirley and Sharon followed him, but Bertie took a minute to take in the beauty and the sadness of the moment. She whispered into the wind, "I'll think of you, Aunt Maddie. You were a good aunt and a good friend to me, and I'll miss you terribly. Just know that you were loved." Then she slowly turned and headed towards the house to join the others.

CHAPTER 2

Mr. Gray sat at the dining room table with Shirley and Sharon. They were surrounded by Aunt Maddie's gleaming antique china on top of credenzas and in a giant breakfront that she had inherited from her mother. Bertie cringed guiltily and silently begged, *"Oh please, don't have left me the china, Aunt Maddie. It's beautiful and all, but what in the world would I do with it? Please, please, please—no china!"*

Mr. Gray cleared his throat and said, "OK, let's get started, shall we?" He started reading, "I, Maddie Maloney, being of sound mind and body…"

Shirley snorted this time, then looked embarrassed, clearly remembering the naked gardening incident. Mr. Gray gave her a stern glance and continued.

"To Shirley Bird, my neighbor. I leave my rose bushes and homemade fertilizer formula. She may move any to her property as thanks for not calling the cops on me several times. She knows what I'm talking about."

Shirley nodded knowingly and then beamed, quite pleased at Aunt Maddie's gift.

Mr. Gray continued, "To Sharon Brown, I leave my antique cookware to add to her collection hanging on the walls of the cafe. This is meant to say thanks for the many meals she brought to me in person. You make the best veggie sandwich in Mississippi, and I appreciated it all very much."

Sharon looked around at the others with delight. "Wonderful!" she cried. "Maddie has some cool stuff. It'll look great in the cafe. Maybe I'll put up a little plaque to remember her by near the display."

Mr. Gray went on, "To my beloved niece, Bertie Ryan, I leave my letters." Surprised, Bertie blinked then looked expectantly at Mr. Gray, waiting for him to continue.

He did continue, but not in the way Bertie expected. "And to the City of Natchez, I leave the remainder of my estate, including my house, to be used as a new public library with the stipulation that there be a well-stocked spirituality and metaphysical section."

"Wow!" said Shirley.

"I didn't see that coming," said Sharon with wide eyes. "Leave it to Maddie to do something unique. The city will love this, of course."

Bertie sat stunned and could not bring herself to say anything. She was in a bit of shock to think that, with all Aunt Maddie's money, and in light of the fondness they had for each other, Maddie only left her some letters. Bertie was hurt. Not that she was after the money. Oh, she could use some funds. Who couldn't? The coffeehouse needed some work on the roof, and the refrigerator units were threatening to die. Bertie just couldn't understand Maddie's reasoning.

When Shirley and Sharon left shortly afterward, Mr. Gray tried to clear up the mystery. "Bertie, your aunt didn't want to saddle you with what she called this 'old rattle trap.'" He smiled and wiped his glasses. Then he handed her two sealed envelopes.

Bertie was still stunned as she took both items from the attorney, who also handed her his card.

"I need to get back to the office now, Ms. Ryan. I know this is all overwhelming, so please don't hesitate to reach out to me with questions." He headed for the door, then turned back and said softly, "I'm afraid I can't leave you here by yourself, as this place and all its contents now legally belong to the city." He held the door open for her.

Bertie felt like she had just been thrown to the curb by a bouncer. She had hoped to wander around the house afterwards, visiting memories of her aunt and her childhood.

Attorney Gray continued, "I'm so sorry. I am. But I have to do things by the letter."

"Sure, sure," said Bertie, as she stumbled down the front steps.

She sat in her car for a long moment. Then she picked up her phone and dialed Della Davis, a part-time chef at a New Orleans po-boy diner, a fiery redhead of fifty-nine years, and her best friend in the world.

When Della answered, Bertie could hear loud diner noises in the background. "I can't really talk right now, but real quick—how did it go?" asked Della bluntly. "And did Aunt Maddie leave you anything good?"

"I'm in shock, Della," said Bertie dazedly. "She left the whole house and everything in it to the city. She left me a couple of letters."

"That's it?" asked Della, astonished.

"Yeah, that's it."

There was a pause. "Girl, those had better be some *damn* good letters!"

CHAPTER 3

Bertie pulled into the driveway of her blue, craftsman-style house on tree-lined Carrollton Avenue. The streetcar route ran down the middle of her street, and its familiar bell was a welcome-home signal. Once inside, she changed into some comfy clothing and curled up on her soft, blue velvet couch. She was surrounded by artwork she had collected from places all over town, from galleries on Julia Street to curbsides on trash day. After the day she'd had, she needed the company of a glass of merlot. A large glass. Full. With her aunt's letter marked "#1" in hand.

It was in a plain, white envelope, nothing fancy. Knowing her frugal aunt, it probably came from the Dollar Store. Classic Aunt Maddie. Bertie didn't know what to expect, but hoped for some sweet parting words from her aunt, maybe a sentimental nod to their bond, as she opened the letter and read:

Well, well, well, Bertie,

If you're reading this, then I'm no longer around to enjoy your company and phone calls, as I have over the years. You know I love you, kid. Always have. Thank you for being such a bright spot in my life.

I suppose you're wondering now why I didn't leave you the treasury. Hehe. Don't be mad. I know you could probably use a few bucks, but believe it or not, I'm leaving you something worth more than the house and everything in it. Besides, I always wanted a library in this part of town. So, that's done.

But, back to you. What I'm about to tell you will sound completely ridiculous, and you are not going to believe it at first. Trust me. You're not. But you will eventually, dear, you will. I didn't believe it at first either, when it happened to me, which wasn't all that long ago. I wanted to do this in person, but I guess, since you're reading this, it didn't work out that way. My plan was to have you over to the house and tell you, but just in case we couldn't make that visit happen, I put everything in this letter as a backup. Okay, here goes.

Bertie, as you are reading this letter, you are being engulfed with a gift. A gift of powers. Yes, that's what I said, and no, I have not gone off the deep end.

During the days and months to follow, strange things will happen to you. You will discover that you can do things you never imagined. Spend this next period experimenting with your powers to see what you can and cannot do. Needless to say, this is going to be interesting!

It was a few years ago when I turned eighty-five and not in the best of health when I was given this gift, so I didn't get to do as much as I would have liked, but you are different. I was told that I must choose my successor to these powers. And so, my dear niece, I choose you. I know you are a good person, Bertie. You're kind, and you have a heart for others. Plus, you have a good support system with those lovely friends of yours. I have faith in you, dear, and you should have it too.

Now, this is important, dear niece. Know that you, too, can give the powers to others, but be careful.

Do it wisely, but do it. I wasn't able to share my powers with but one person. The person of my choice—you, of course. But it will be different for you. I believe you were chosen to share and that the sharing will start a new phase of human evolution. Yes, just a little thing like that!

Also, the powers have rules and in the wrong hands can be a pain in the ass, but also fun! (You saw the roses, right?)

You have a lot to learn now, dear. Be patient, and be kind. Learning to use the powers is kind of a test—a checks and balances type of thing—to make sure that you are the right keeper of this gift. But I know you are.

Hopefully, I'll get to watch the show from wherever it is I'm going. I hope they have margaritas!! Hehe

Love, love, love, and kisses, my dear,
Aunt Maddie

"Oh, Aunt Maddie, I miss you," Bertie said aloud to her empty living room. Then she sighed. "Poor thing must have lost her marbles at the end. Probably dementia kicking in."

She felt awful as she pictured Maddie rattling around that big house, thinking she had superpowers, with no one to help her. The guilt hit hard. Bertie wiped away a tear.

She eyed the second letter, thinking, *"I'll bet it's filled with more nonsense. Well, I'm not going to let this get out to anyone. Aunt Maddie needs to be remembered with some dignity. It's the least I can do now."*

She suddenly felt overwhelmed by all the events of the day, not to mention the pure grief she felt over her aunt. She left the letters on the coffee table and went to run a hot bath.

CHAPTER 4

The next morning, Della called early and found Bertie lounging in her Adirondack chair, sipping coffee on the back porch. Live oaks framed her view of her lush backyard.

"OK," Della said, without preamble. "Catch me up. Was the drive home okay? The funeral service? And what's in those letters?"

Bertie chuckled. Classic Della. "The drive was fine. The service was…odd. Just two other women, her neighbor, the local cafe owner, and her attorney were there. Aunt Maddie had some weird relationships, if you can call them that. She left each of the two women a little something, the letters went to me, of course, and everything else—and I mean everything else—went to the city. Honestly, yes, I'm weirded out by it, but I'm also a little relieved. If she had left me the house and everything, I would have lost my mind trying to figure out what to do with it all. I know what to do with the letters."

"Oh dear, you didn't throw them out, did you?" teased Della.

Bertie chuckled. "No, no. Nothing like that. I haven't even read the second one."

"What did the first letter say?"

Bertie hesitated. She usually told Della everything, but she thought, *I see no reason to share Aunt Maddie's crazy last days. Della met Aunt Maddie a few years back and loved her too. And she loved my stories about growing up around that quirky woman. No, no. There's no point in spoiling Della's opinion of dear Aunt Maddie.*

She answered, "Just said that she loved me, and that I was her favorite. That sort of thing." It was only half a lie.

"Yeah, Maddie always did have her own way of doing things, didn't she?" Della went on, "Well, listen, I was also calling to tell you that the book club meets this week at the coffeehouse as usual, and they are hoping you'll have time to cook up a batch of your jambalaya for lunch."

Bertie chuckled. "What part of the word coffeehouse do you not understand? We serve coffee, remember?"

"Oh, you know you love to cook for us," teased Della.

Bertie had to smile because her friend knew her so well. It was true that she did love to cook for her friends and occasionally served them lunch at the coffeehouse when they met for book club. But it always confused her customers on those days when they walked in expecting the warm aroma of good coffee and discovered the spicy smell of simmering shrimp jambalaya. She always ended up serving the customers some too.

"OK, sure thing. Just text me when they confirm a day. I'll make a pot."

"Will do. Okay, gotta run now. Hair appointment. This red hair doesn't dye itself, you know."

Bertie chuckled as she hung up and leaned back. She breathed in the warm southern air. Her eyes drifted to a flower pot near the steps where she had planted some peas, hoping they would climb up the porch railing. She grimaced when she looked in the pot and saw that nothing had sprouted.

"Shoot," she said to the peas. "I was really hoping they would grow. My mom always had porch peas when I was a kid." She sighed. She could picture the beautiful, fresh peas growing up the railings long ago. She remembered how sweet those new peas tasted when she pinched one from her mom's crop.

She glanced into her empty coffee cup and sighed again, *It's a two-cup day, for sure.* She headed to the kitchen and the coffee pot.

A few minutes later, she was back out and about to take the first sip when her eye caught on the pot of newly planted peas she had been lamenting over just minutes ago. Bertie froze. The pot had been empty. Now, it was full of pea vines nearly a foot tall. And they were still growing.

Her coffee cup slipped from her hand, shattering on the wooden porch. She hardly noticed. The pea plants were wrapping around the railing, pushing out fresh pods before her eyes.

She blinked, trying to clear her vision, and thought, *"Okaaay… so this is how it starts. This is dementia or some other horror like it. Next, I'll be seeing flying saucers and aliens dancing in the yard. Good Lord! They're gonna put me away for sure!"*

No matter how long she stared, the plants kept growing. She was not imagining this.

She suddenly remembered what her aunt's letter had said: "Strange things will happen." She ran for the second envelope. *"Oh, good lord! Where is that other letter?"*

CHAPTER 5

Bertie snatched the second letter off the coffee table, hands trembling as she tore it open. Her aunt's unmistakable scrawl greeted her on the first page.

Bertie,

Ha! Hold onto your hat, girl. We're just getting started!

This second letter goes with the first one. The following are copies of some journal entries I wrote when I first got the powers. I wasn't much of a journal keeper, and there are only two entries, but I think they might help you as you are starting out with the gift. So here goes:

* ~ *

Journal Entry 1 – Maddie Maloney – age 85

Is this real, or is this the imaginings of a crazy old woman? I mean me, of course. It all started yesterday when I visited Gladys Yurt in the hospital. She and I are the last two from our primary school still breathing. Gladys' ticker is giving out, and I got my neighbor, Shirley, to drive me to the hospital to say goodbye. I wouldn't have gone for just anyone—I don't get out much these days—but Gladys and I were thick as thieves when we were girls.

Oh, and she was a hoot back then. She's the one who dared me to kiss Joe Heffernan back in first grade. I did it, too. Kissed him right by the monkey bars. Then ran off before he even knew what hit him. Those were fun days, but Gladys and I drifted apart when we went to different high schools. We both still live in town, however, and bump into each other now and then. I don't have many friends left, so I made the trip to the hospital.

Gladys was in pretty rough shape when we visited. Her white hair was cut short and kind of a mess, and she couldn't have weighed more than ninety pounds. But we still had a good visit—at first. We were chatting a bit about old times and our gardens. I was in the middle of rambling about hydrangeas when something weird happened. And I mean weird.

Gladys suddenly grabbed my hand.

"Maddie, I have something to tell you."

I stopped talking about the flowers. Gladys sat up in bed a little (no small feat in her condition.) Her voice was serious.

"Maddie, we both know I don't have a lot of time left, and I must tell you something."

I couldn't imagine what she had to say. That she forgot to turn off her iron? That she'd robbed the Midtown bank and wanted to confess? That she stole my eighth-grade boyfriend, John Beesom? (I already knew that, by the way. I didn't really like him anyway.) What could it be?

Gladys went on, "I'm giving you my powers, Maddie. There, it's done." Then she plopped back against her pillows again.

I didn't say anything for a moment because I figured I couldn't have heard her right. Or the poor old dear was off her noggin. "I'm sorry, Gladys, but you're giving me your what now?"

"My powers. It's done. You've got them now."

I started to change the subject because, honestly, I didn't know what to say to something like that. I mean, think about it. It's not something you hear every day, and chances are the person saying it isn't swimming in the right lane. I figured she must be delirious. But she looked at me with that old familiar fire in her eyes.

"Maddie, just listen. You are the one I've been waiting for these many years. And the one the world has been waiting for—for centuries. The gift of powers was passed down to me, and now I've passed them on to you. They are holy powers, Maddie. Use them for mankind's highest good. Learn by doing, just like I did. And just as I did, you will need to guard them till you find your one successor, and that person will be the one to awaken the world. Very shortly, odd things will begin to happen to you. You will begin to experience these powers and a shift in awareness. You'll become more joyful, and you'll feel a connection to something larger than yourself, and so much more.

Gladys kept babbling about how the gift was sacred, and she kept mentioning things that didn't make sense to me at the time—things about raising human consciousness and saving the world. She told me to study those topics, but honestly, at that time, I didn't understand what she was talking about. She was rambling and ranting.

I tried to interrupt her and laugh it off. "Oh, c'mon, Gladys," I told her. "We're a bit too old for this kind of joking around, don't you think?"

"You're telling me," Gladys laughed, but I could tell she was serious. And tiring fast. She went on softly, "Nevertheless, it will happen as I say. We can talk more about this tomorrow when you come back. Everything in your life will be different by then."

Her eyes fluttered shut, but she still mumbled, "Oh, thank God, I found you, Maddie. It's taken me forever to find my chosen person. And it was you all along. So, I did my job, and I know you will too. Just remember, be smart, pay attention, stay loving, and learn. The world is counting on you."

A nurse came in then, shooing me out gently so that Gladys could rest.

I got to my feet, and I remember thinking, "Well, I wasn't planning on coming back tomorrow, but I'll try to talk Shirley into it." I whispered "See you later, Gladys" to my old friend and went downstairs to meet Shirley, who was waiting in the lobby.

I was feeling pretty wrung-out myself as we drove home, but I managed to convince Shirley that we needed to return the next day.

That evening, I was watering my roses in the backyard, fussing over one spindly, little bush in particular. I gave it a good watering of my special blend of rose food and a pep talk. It went something like, "C'mon, little rose bush, grow big and strong. I know you can do it. I can just see you now as the most magnificent bush in the garden. Your roses will be huge and pearlescent white, your leaves bright, waxy green and glorious, your stems strong, and your sweet fragrance will stop passersby in their tracks." I pictured how it could grow and outshine all the other roses in the garden.

Then, I called it a night and went inside for my supper, a little TV, and then to bed.

The next morning, I got out of bed and stood in front of the window, stretching while I took off my nightgown. But before I could manage to pull on my day clothes, something in the garden caught my eye. I had to squint because what I was seeing didn't make sense. I said, "What in the world is that?? Did someone plant a magnolia tree out back overnight?"

I was so bewildered and curious that I bolted downstairs without my shoes. Without my pants and top either! Straight out the back door. I slowed down as I got nearer to the little, struggling rose bush that I'd talked to the evening before, and thought, "What is happening here?"

I was gobsmacked. Truly. And I'm not sure I've ever been truly gobsmacked before. That spindly, little rose bush had grown to a magnificent size with white blossoms as large as dinner plates.

I walked around and around it, expecting some sort of joke or at least an explanation, but I was getting nothing.

I threw my arms in the air in a mix of frustration and awe—when I heard a voice.

"Uh, good morning, Maddie. Everything alright?"

It was Shirley peeking over the fence. That's when I realized I was stark naked.

I cleared my throat. Somehow, I knew not to mention the roses to Shirley, but it left me in a pickle about why I was bum-naked in the garden. I gathered my dignity and called out, "Fine day for sunbathing, don't you think?" I strode past her, head held high, calling behind me, "See you later for that trip to the hospital."

When I got inside, I slammed the door and just leaned against it for a minute or two. My heart was racing, and I was a little out of breath. That didn't seem like a good thing for an eighty-five-year-old, so I just stayed there for quite a while with my eyes closed, trying to slow my breath. But my mind was racing too. I thought, "Those roses were real! I saw them with my own two old eyes. Is this what Gladys meant by powers? Is she trying to kill me? Something like this could stop a person's heart!"

I turned and peeked through the glass window in the door at the garden. "Yep, it's still there!"

I marched upstairs to get dressed, and I said out loud, "Gladys Yurt, you have some big-time explaining to do!"

CHAPTER 6

Bertie closed her eyes for a moment. Her aunt's journal entry was wild. Unbelievable. Yet there were peas growing right in front of her face. She needed to take a break and go to the kitchen for another cup of coffee, just to give her time to wrap her mind around what she'd read so far. But she couldn't put the letter down and dove back in.

Journal Entry 2 – Maddie Maloney

I needed to get back to the hospital to see Gladys. All morning, I stared out the window at those monster roses, wondering what I'd done. Were these the powers Gladys mentioned?

Shirley drove me again later that morning. When we arrived at the hospital, I hurried out of the car as fast as this eighty-five-year-old body would move. Shirley huffed and puffed behind me, hollering, "Where's the fire, Maddie? Wait up!"

I slowed down grudgingly, but when the elevator opened onto the third floor, I scooted through the doors and down the hall. When I reached Gladys' room, I saw that her door was wide open, and so I called out as I swung into the room. "Gladys, it's Maddie!"

But instead of my old friend, a young woman in scrubs stood in her place.

I was out of breath, but asked, "Where did they move Gladys?"

By this time, Shirley had caught up and was looking around the room.

The young nurse asked me. "Are you family to Miss Gladys?"

"Might as well be," I told her firmly. "I've known her all my life."

The nurse's face softened. "I'm so sorry. I sure wish I had better news for you, but Miss Gladys passed away last night."

The words hit me like a punch. I staggered, and Shirley grabbed my arm.

"Oh no, Poor Gladys! I so wanted to talk to her again."

Shirley patted my arm. "Maddie, I'm so sorry about your friend. At least you got to say goodbye."

I snapped back, "You wouldn't say that if you knew what I knew."

Shirley gave me a strange look, and I quickly added, "I mean, our friendship meant a lot to me."

Shirley nodded sympathetically. "Let's get you home,"

Back at the house, I had to convince Shirley that I was fine so that she would leave. Then, I sat in the parlor, stunned. My mind was racing.

"Poor Gladys. She's gone, and I'm going to miss her."

But, one moment I sat grieving my old friend, and then the next moment, I was thinking, "Oh my good lord, what about these powers? I'm gonna die and kill that Gladys when I catch up to her. What has she done to me?"

A thought suddenly occurred to me. "Maybe it was all just a fluke—a one-time thing. A weird coincidence. Maybe these silly 'powers' are gone. Maybe they even left when Gladys passed on."

There was only one way to find out. I tried to remember what I had done with the rosebush to make it go crazy in my garden. I recalled that I had spoken to it, pictured it as healthy and growing, and then watered it lovingly.

As I wandered into the kitchen, trying to remember everything, my stomach growled. With all the excitement of the morning, I had forgotten to eat breakfast. I must have been in such a state, because I'm never not hungry. I thought longingly of avocado toast with a squeeze of lemon. Too bad I was out of avocados, not to mention that the toaster was on the fritz. I would just have to cook something else, although eggs or oatmeal just didn't sound as good.

Still, I imagined it so clearly, I could taste it. I shrugged, and I headed upstairs to get out of my good, blue dress and into some day clothes before cooking. When I came back downstairs and went to the kitchen, I took two steps onto the black and white linoleum floor and stopped dead in my tracks.

There it was. A perfect plate of avocado toast sat on the counter. Garnished with a cherry tomato and capers.

I sat down slowly on a barstool and put my hand to my forehead, reeling in astonishment and confusion. After a minute, I calmed down and shook my head.

"OK. The rosebush was not a one-time trick. I don't know what I'm going to do about it, though." I looked at the warm toast in front of me and thought, "Is this even real toast?" I poked it and felt the soft bread texture, and then took a sniff. "Is that lemon juice? That's just the way I like it!"

I shrugged, thinking, "No point in wasting good food." Even if it had materialized from thin air, I took a bite. Heavenly. I wasn't going to let a little thing like superpowers stop me from enjoying a good breakfast.

"Gladys, old girl, what in the world have you gotten me into?"

Bertie, that is all I have in the way of a journal, but I hope it helped you, dear.

Just as Bertie got to the end of the journal entry, her phone buzzed. It was Della.

"Hey, what's up?" Bertie answered, still shaken by Maddie's journal.

"The book club decided that tomorrow is the best day for everyone to meet at the Bump and Grind. Does that work for you for the jambalaya too?"

"Oh sure, sure," she said distractedly. Then, recovering slightly, she teased, "I'll be happy to cook for the girls. You'll be lucky if I don't eat it all myself before you get there."

All the women looked forward to the monthly book club. It was the one time all month that Bertie allowed herself time off from running the coffeehouse, except for nearly daily phone calls from Della.

The Bookies, as they called their group, had been meeting for over eight years and had settled into a routine of eating Bertie's comforting food and reading books about topics they loved. Sometimes they chose history, and other times it was the classics. But mostly, they read books about spirituality and consciousness-raising. Bertie couldn't wait to hear what the group thought of the latest book choice.

Della asked, "Want me to come early and help?"

"Wouldn't hurt," said Bertie. "I'm having quite a week and could use a hand."

"You mean because of your aunt's passing and all?"

"Well, yes…" Bertie started to say, then hesitated, wondering, *"Is it a good idea to share the news about the powers with people?"* She didn't know. *"Wouldn't everyone think I was nuts? Even Della?"*

She smiled to herself. And thought, *"Probably, but I mean, so peas grew on the porch. Is that a reason to go berserk? Maybe it is, and maybe it's not."* Then she decided, *"No, I don't think I should tell anyone about this yet. I need to think."*

CHAPTER 7

The Bump and Grind was a repurposed old house on Maple Street in New Orleans, four blocks from Bertie's house. Bertie had painted the coffeehouse a cheerful blue with yellow awnings and orange trim. Bright yellow outdoor umbrellas lifted customers' spirits as they walked up the old concrete steps to the front porch. The interior was filled with warm colors and bright, healthy plants, along with the heavenly aroma of Bertie's good coffee and pastries. In the front corner stood an old upright piano that Bertie had rescued and revitalized. Occasionally, a customer would take a turn at the keys, much to the delight of the regulars. Bertie's best friend Della, was a talented pianist, and she often livened the place with ragtime numbers from her repertoire.

On the day of the book club meeting, Della was the first of the Bookies to arrive at the coffeehouse. Her curly red hair was in a scrunchy and formed a frizzy fountain on top of her head. Her slim figure was covered in her usual attire—jeans and boots. Bertie called it her uniform, but it suited Della's casual approach to clothes and life perfectly.

The tantalizing aroma of Bertie's shrimp jambalaya filled the cafe, prompting customers to request it at nearly every table. Good thing Bertie had made a big batch for the Bookies. She'd learned that lesson long ago.

She immediately put Della to work setting up the Bookie's usual table in the staff's private lunch room. She handed Della folded sets of utensils wrapped in napkins, along with condiments and glasses of ice water for the table. Meanwhile, Bertie hovered over the stove, stirring the jambalaya so it wouldn't scorch.

She decided to add just a smidge more salt when she realized that she couldn't reach it. It had been moved across the room to the kitchen island. She hesitated, not wanting to leave the pot unattended. Then a crazy thought popped into her head. At this point, she had spent the better part of the previous night thinking about Aunt Maddie and trying out her new, bizarre inheritance. She still wasn't quite sure she believed it was true. She decided to test it again. She looked at the big spoon in her hand and got a picture in her mind. She spoke these words out loud, "Stir this pot, spoon." To her amazement and slight horror, the spoon leapt out of her hand and began to do the job. It rose, dipped, and circled through the jambalaya like it had a mind of its own. Bertie gawked. Snapping out of her daze, she dashed across the room for the salt.

Just as she turned back to the stove, Della burst in looking for extra napkins. She froze, staring at the dancing spoon.

"What—the—heck?" was all she managed to stutter out.

Bertie sprang forward as quickly as a cat and snatched the spoon from mid-air. As Della stood in shock, Bertie got very busy all of a sudden. She flipped off the burner and moved the pot to a cool spot on the stove. "There, that's done now," she said. Her head throbbed with tension.

Thinking fast, she grabbed a dish towel and started shooing Della out of the kitchen,

"Let's go! The girls will be here any minute. Chop-chop!"

Della blinked at her. "Bertie…"

But Bertie cut her off. "I gotta get this jambalaya on the table."

"But…"

"Sorry, can't talk now. Busy, busy, busy!" chattered Bertie, refusing to meet her friend's eye.

Della stared, her arms crossed with a look for her friend that said, *I'm not buying this for one second.* But, as luck would have it, the rest of the Bookies began to arrive in full force, pulling Della out of the confrontation and back into the dining room.

Bertie hustled to get bowls of jambalaya out to them. As she set the final bowl on the table, Della grabbed her arm and hissed, "I saw what I saw, Bertie. This is not over."

CHAPTER 8

The Bookies dove into their food as soon as Bertie sat down, strategically placing herself as far away from Della as possible. Every time she dared glance up, Della was glaring at her over a spoonful of jambalaya.

After a lunch filled with satisfied sighs, groans of pleasure, and compliments, the five women were eager to begin a discussion of their latest read.

The group included Bertie, Della, and three other women. There was Bonnie, a retired schoolteacher who had joined a knitting group recently, and always wore something she had knitted to the Bookies' meeting, even in the blistering summer. She always carried a bag full of knitted potholders to give out wherever she went.

Next Sue, who worked part-time taking care of horses on a ranch across the river. Her healthy tan and huge grin always made her a welcoming sight.

And finally, there was Cathy, a retired nurse battling stage three breast cancer, who now spent more time at doctors' appointments than almost anywhere else. "I'm so happy to see y'all," she said, smiling. She was doing her best to live a normal life while undergoing treatments. Meeting with the Bookies meant so much to her, and her gratitude showed in her beautiful smile.

Cathy began the book discussion. "Wasn't this a great read? It's so interesting to read how quantum physics is related to spirituality. It's fascinating."

Sue added, "Mind-blowing stuff. The idea that our consciousness can affect our surroundings, and that thoughts can shape reality. It sounds like, if that's true, then our thoughts and consciousness can literally change the world."

Bonnie, picking up her knitting, chimed in, "So, theoretically, if we all raise our consciousness together, then mankind can shift into a reality dictated by love instead of separation. Just imagine that! And, by the way, not to change the subject, but would anyone like a new potholder?"

In perfect harmony, the Bookies, who all had too many of Bonnie's potholders as it was, answered, "No!"

Bonnie sniffed and frowned, but continued knitting one anyway.

Sue picked up where they left off, " Imagine the joy if people actually did this. People would be so much happier."

Della, finally peeling her eyes off Bertie, said, "It seems to me that raising our consciousness is one of the most important things human beings can do."

"Well, the author does give practical tips on how it can be done. Meditation and spending time in nature—those sorts of things."

"Here's what I was thinking," said Sue. "What if groups like ours started doing that together? Little pockets of people meditating together might affect a big change."

The women around the table looked at each other, surprised. Bertie asked, "You mean like meditating at our book club meetings?"

Sue shrugged. "Why not? It might be worth a try."

Della grinned at her friend. "I like it, Bookies!"

"It sure couldn't hurt," added Cathy, quietly looking down at her lap, starting to feel a bit unwell from her last treatment. "Maybe raising our consciousness can promote some healing."

There was a gentle silence as their focus shifting to Cathy.

"There have been many documented cases of people being healed through meditations and energy work," Bertie offered.

Cathy nodded, "Even traditional doctors tell their patients to think positively. They don't know why exactly, but they know it helps."

"So, what do y'all think?" asked Bertie. "Do you want to try it? We could do it before or after each meeting. This little room is quiet enough that we can play some meditation music here. Maybe we can focus on an outcome during each meditation. Have a group intention like world peace, or perhaps a healing?"

All their eyes turned towards Cathy, questioning.

Sue spoke up, "Would you be okay with us trying it out on you, Cathy?"

Tears welled in Cathy's eyes. "I would love that. Just being surrounded by you girls lifts my heart."

"That settles it, then," said Della, fiddling with her phone to find the right music.

Bonnie added, "I think visualization is the important key to this. So, let's all visualize Cathy being healed, happy, and living her best life."

The Bookies agreed, and for the next twenty minutes, the women sat with their backs straight, eyes closed, hands in their laps, and meditated on Cathy's healing.

Bertie pictured her friend glowing with health, full-haired, smiling, and strolling breezily down the street in her signature colorful leggings and a yellow t-shirt. Bertie smiled at the idea, then thought, *"How odd that they had picked this particular book. A book about raising consciousness. Bertie had a hard time believing in coincidences. Maybe this was another one of those things that Aunt Maddie was talking about when she said strange things would start to happen."*

When they were done meditating, Cathy said quietly, "Thanks, Bookies. You know I love all y'all."

The women hugged Cathy and then made a pact to continue the practice at every meeting. As they began packing up, chatting about their next read, Bertie quietly slipped away.

Della lingered until the last woman left, then headed back to the kitchen.

The only person there was Bertie's dishwasher, Eddie.

"Eddie, where's Bertie?"

He shut off the faucet, stuck a thumb out towards the back door, and said, "She left. Said something about a doctor's appointment."

Disgusted, Della turned back to the front exit, muttering, "Doctor's appointment, my ass. Okay, no problem. I will catch up with her tomorrow. Like I said, this is not over."

CHAPTER 9

For two days, Bertie ghosted Della. No texts. No calls. Nothing. She felt like she was lying low after robbing a bank. Instead of facing the world—or her best friend—she hunkered down at home, spinning with confusion, awe, and not a small dose of anxiety over her new powers. She needed to think. She even called in sick to the coffeehouse, an almost unheard-of occurrence.

The powers from Aunt Maddie were real. Too real. And Bertie didn't know what to make of them, and she had no one to talk to about them.

Over those two days, she tested her abilities carefully. Craving Quiche Lorraine before lunch, she closed her eyes and pictured it—golden, savory, and waiting in her fridge. Sure enough, at noon, there it was, still warm and delicious.

Feeling bolder, and cheeky, she imagined logging into her bank account and discovering an extra cool million. With that thought, she practically ran to her computer.

Nothing.

"Shoot," she muttered, "Same old balance." And it sure wasn't a million dollars.

"Hmmm, I'll bet this means something important about the powers," she thought.

That evening, she spotted her elderly neighbor, Mr. Fielding, in his yard with his walker. On a whim, she imagined him finding a box on his front porch with a luscious chocolate cake inside. She bet that he would love that. She waited, but didn't see any boxes appear on his porch. Just to make sure, she waved to him and asked. "Hey, Mr. Fielding, how's it going today?"

"I've been better, Bertie. My doctor upped my insulin again. Been feeling off, and now I know why. It's so hard to watch my diet so closely. I have a terrible sweet tooth!"

Bertie winced, *"Oh dear, thank goodness that cake didn't appear. If he'd gotten hold of it, I could have put the poor man in the hospital! I guess I can't go wishing for things willy-nilly. They could have consequences."*

"Hmmmm," her mind was humming. *"Maybe it didn't happen because it would have caused harm. And perhaps that's why I didn't get my million bucks. It was self-serving and perhaps would have come to no good."* She puzzled over it for a while. *"But, wait a minute, the quiche was self-serving too."* She concluded that a quiche would not cause any harm, but a million dollars, if acquired greedily or not used properly, or if it influenced someone in the wrong way, just might cause a lot of harm. *"Lesson learned. Don't manifest recklessly. Some things have consequences."*

Delighted, Bertie realized that the powers needed to be used for good, and there seemed to be safeguards that made it so. *"And if that's true and your wish didn't come true, even with good intentions, it was because there were harmful repercussions you weren't aware of."* She understood she'd have to trust that because a person couldn't see all the repercussions of their actions, like Mr. Fielding's chocolate cake. The powers would prevent her from doing harm. Having faith in that brought Bertie a sense of relief.

That night, to soothe her spinning thoughts, she envisioned a gentle rain to help her fall asleep and was rewarded with soft patter against her windows. Smiling, she drifted off to sleep, comforted by the certainty that the flowers—and maybe she—were in good hands.

CHAPTER 10

The following morning, Bertie fished a letter from Attorney Michael Gray out of the mailbox on her front porch.

"Now what?" she thought worriedly, as she tore it open.

Dear Ms. Ryan:

Following instructions from your Aunt Maddie, I mailed this third letter to you from your aunt the day after her funeral services. Please contact me if you require my services.

Michael Gray

Bertie rifled through the pages and began reading:

Bertie, dear—surprise!

It's been a few days since you've received the powers, and hopefully you are getting the hang of them. Have you figured out the rules yet? Don't worry. You will as you go along. That's part of the learning process. The main thing to remember is that you must use your powers for good.

And not just for good, Oh Lord—so much more than that! It took me a few years to figure this out, and I didn't want to spring this on you in the first letter because, Bertie, it's a lot. But you are up to the task. I just know you are. Here's the deal—the powers are not just a gift for doing parlor tricks and making pretty roses. The gift is a responsibility. Bertie. And, if you haven't guessed it by now, it is divine – straight from Source. I believe it is God taking a hand in the next step of human evolution. And thank God for that! We could use the help!

The responsibility is that you must use the powers to raise mankind's consciousness. Yes, just a little thing like the whole earth's consciousness! It's time, Bertie, and it's up to you. The world is at a tipping point, and you are part of the solution. It will happen within your lifetime.

So, here's a quick lesson on consciousness:

Bertie was taken aback. She had never discussed this topic with her aunt, but it was the very subject that was the center of her book club's discussions and reading choice. Fascinated, Bertie kept reading

Study up on the topic, Bertie. They will help guide you in this mission of yours. And make no mistake—it is a mission. Okay, here goes nothing—and with lots of bullet points!

• ***Let's start with dimensions.***

Think of dimensions as levels of consciousness – of reality - like channels on a radio.

The third dimension (3D) is physical, based in time, space, and separation- it's where mankind is now.

The fourth (4D) is a transitional phase—filled with thought, emotion, and awakening.

The fifth (5D) is unity, joy, love, higher truth, and manifestations. It's where we remember who we really are. It's where we want to go right now.

There are higher dimensions than the fifth one, leading us closer and closer to the divine, but once we get to the fifth, the others will be reached more easily.

• **Let's talk about the Third Dimension.** *The world lives in the third dimension. How do we know? Because it checks all the following boxes of the third dimension outlined by scholars, such as:*

- *Separation feels real.*
  You see yourself as separate from others, nature, and even the divine.
  It's "me vs. them," "this vs. that," "good vs. bad."
- *Fear runs the show. Worry, control, competition, and survival drive our choices.*
  There's a constant low hum of anxiety about money, aging, worth, and success.
- *Time is rigid. You feel trapped by clocks, schedules, and deadlines.*
  The past defines you. The future worries you. The present feels elusive.
- *Identity is external. You define yourself by what you do, what you own, or what others think. You may say things like: "I'll be happy when..." or, "I'm not enough."*
- *Conflict is common. You find yourself judging, comparing, or trying to "win."*
  Peace feels temporary, like it can be lost at any moment. And it can.
- *You feel stuck. Life feels like a grind. Like you're doing a lot, but not really being.*

- *You might ask yourself, "Is this all there is?" The answer is "No. There is so much more."*

We all start in 3D, Bertie. It's part of the human journey. But once you notice it...you're already beginning to move beyond it. Awareness is the doorway to higher dimensions.

• So, what is consciousness?

Consciousness is awareness—your ability to observe, feel, choose, and be.

It expands the more you let go of fear, judgment, and ego.

What determines our dimension or level of consciousness?

Frequency.

Everything vibrates—emotions, thoughts, even your body.

Fear, anger, and shame are low frequencies.

Love, peace, and joy are high frequencies.

Your frequency is like your soul's radio signal— it attracts what matches. Frequencies determine your dimension, so if we want to raise our level of consciousness, we must raise our frequency level. Joy is a powerful frequency! Tune in, then turn it up so others can find it too.

• Why Shift from 3D to 5D:

- *3D is built on survival, conflict, and scarcity. It keeps us stuck.*
- *In 5D, we operate from compassion, joy, unity, and creation, not control.*

- *Moving to 5D is how we heal ourselves, our relationships, and the world.*

• How do we raise our consciousness from 3D to 5D?
- *Practice presence. Breathe. Come back to the now.*
- *Let go of needing to be right. Choose peace.*
- *Feel your feelings fully, then release them.*
- *Follow joy—it's the compass to your higher self.*
- *Meditate, create, forgive, and love yourself first, then others.*

• So, what is the gift/your new powers?

They allow you to begin your shift from 3D to 5D and to share that ability with others. Shifting into 5D is a process, and manifesting isn't something that usually happens immediately. So, this is a "bump up" in the process. Humanity needs a little help right now, and Bertie, you are the catalyst.

You're already on the path, dear. Just keep walking forward. Source has your back.

Love from a fellow traveler—and your favorite aunt,
Maddie

CHAPTER 11

The next morning, Bertie woke up to find that her phone, which she had placed on silent mode, had been lighting up like a slot machine since the night before. There were a dozen texts and missed calls.

All from Della.

But she wasn't ready for the barrage yet. She brushed her teeth, poured her coffee, and tried to brace herself.

Then the doorbell rang, not once but three times in a row. "Gee, I wonder who that could be?" Bertie muttered, rolling her eyes. "Hold on, Della, I'm coming."

She hurried to the door and cracked it open. Della bulldozed her way inside.

"Girl, do you seriously think you can avoid me forever?"

"Well, no," quipped Bertie. "Not forever,"

Della's eyes were wild. "Bertie, you're missing everything! You're not going to believe what happened!"

"Then tell me,"

"If you had answered your phone, you'd know already." Della folded her arms with a stubborn frown.

"Are you seriously going to make me beg?"

"That's the idea," said Della with a smirk.

Bertie sighed dramatically. "Fine. Oh Della, Keeper of All Gossip, Ruler of Secrets—please, do tell me what I missed."

Della unfolded her arms, vibrating with excitement, and gushed, "Aside from the fact that my best friend pulled some wild mystical trick that I can't explain for the life of me and then vanished for two days, I've got news. But, believe me, we will be circling back to that mystical stunt when I'm finished!"

"Yeah, yeah," said Bertie, cringing. She was dreading that conversation.

"OK," said Della, barely able to contain herself. "You're not going to believe it. You remember at book club when we meditated together for Cathy's healing?"

Bertie leaned in curiously. "Yes…?"

"Oh my God, Bertie! It worked. Cathy went to the doctor and got her latest tests back yesterday. The tests came back clean! The cancer is gone!"

Bertie's jaw dropped.

"Cathy says she feels great. It's a miracle! And all the Bookies are coming over to the Bump and Grind in a little while to talk about it."

Bertie sank onto the couch, stunned. "Holy smoke. Cathy must be over the moon…and I am too." Berties mind was spinning. *"Did I have something to do with that? Did the powers heal Cathy?"* The idea was overwhelming. She hadn't imagined that she could use her new abilities to cure someone.

Della narrowed her eyes. "I'm not saying that it was just the meditation. But I think you had something to do with it."

Bertie looked at her friend and took a deep breath. "Della, the truth is, I think I did too."

Della jumped to her feet. "I knew it! I don't get it, and if I hadn't seen that pot stirring itself, I would say we're both nuts. But we're not, are we?"

"Honestly, that's still up for debate," said Bertie. "I never thought I'd say this, but no, we're not crazy."

"Start talking, Bertie."

"You're not gonna believe it. I barely believe it myself. I'm afraid that Aunt Maddie left me something much more than a couple of letters." She told Della everything—from the letters to the peas growing, the quiche, and the rain. All of it.

Della's eyes kept widening. "So, you're telling me that you're like Superwoman now?"

"Well, kryptonite won't kill me, and I can't fly," Bertie quipped. Then she frowned. "I don't think so anyway. I probably shouldn't assume anything at this point!"

"How did your aunt give you those powers in the first place?" asked Della.

"I've given that a lot of thought. I think she pictured me having them before she passed, then placed that intention into the letter. When I read it, something clicked, and it activated."

"Wait a minute here…does this mean that you can give other people powers like your aunt gave to you?"

Bertie blinked. "Good Lord! I forgot about that! Aunt Maddie mentioned something about it in her letter!"

"There's one way to find out," said Della, raising her eyebrows questioningly.

"Oh, Della, do you think we should? I'm not sure what I'm supposed to do with all this. We have to be careful. There could be consequences. One thing I know is that the powers need to be used for positive outcomes, or else they just don't work."

The two of them were quiet for a moment. Then Della said thoughtfully, "So wait, if you try to give me the powers and it works, it will be because of a positive outcome. If not, it just won't work, right?"

"That makes sense," said Bertie, nodding slowly, then moaned, "I feel like this is such a huge responsibility. It's just too huge to wrap my mind around."

"I can see how you'd feel like that," said Della. "But don't you think that this is something you couldn't control even if you wanted to? Didn't your aunt say that she believed that you were the one chosen to do something with the powers? What if what you're supposed to do is to share them? That right there might be your mission, Bertie."

"Della, old friend," Bertie laughed. "You can be awfully smart sometimes. It's unsettling."

"Thanks a lot. So, what do you think? Are we in this together?"

"I think we might just be," said Bertie. "OK, let's do it."

"One question first."

"Shoot," said Bertie.

"Can I carry a magic wand?"

"Absolutely. And I'll get a pointy black hat."

Della got a twinkle in her eye and teased her friend. "Are you positive your aunt picked the right person for all this?"

"Not even a little," Bertie said. "C'mon, let's get this done, shall we?"

Della sat up straight on the couch and shut her eyes. Bertie did the same and pictured Della glowing with a golden light, sitting in a garden under tall trees. A dragonfly landed lightly on her hand. A spiral appeared in the other. The whole vision lasted only a few seconds, and then it cleared.

Della opened her eyes to what would slowly become a whole different reality.

CHAPTER 12

After an hour or two of Bertie helping Della cautiously test her new powers, which included Della manifesting Bloody Marys for both of them, the two women strolled down Carrollton Avenue to the coffeehouse to meet the Bookies.

"Bertie, aside from being excited and knowing that I can conjure up a great cocktail, I don't really feel any different. Did you?"

"I didn't either. Not at first," Bertie replied. "I do notice that you have a slight glow to you, though. I think it might be from the powers. Do you notice that about me, too?"

Della peered at her friend. "Now that you mention it, yes. I think that you are glowing even more than I am. Maybe it gets stronger as it goes along."

"You know, I thought Aunt Maddie had gone completely batty when I first read her letter. It was upsetting. Then came a bit of anxiety after the peas started growing. But little by little, I've noticed that I'm calmer and happier. I've become more accepting. Of everything, really. Even giving a lunatic like you superpowers."

They both laughed, years of friendship wrapped in the teasing.

As they walked, Della grew quiet, clearly concentrating. Bertie suspected that her friend was trying out her powers again. Moments later, Bertie discovered a huge bouquet sticking out of her tote bag.

"Well, would you look at that!" Bertie grinned.

"Check out the pink daisies in that bouquet. I invented those— thought they'd be fun." Bertie sniffed at the flowers. "They smell like lemons!"

"Nice touch, right?" her friend asked modestly.

At that moment, a car screeched around the corner, narrowly missing the two women.

"Watch out!" Bertie shouted as both women jumped back.

Della stared after the car, furious.

"Della, are you alright?" asked Bertie, worriedly.

Della lifted her arm and pointed at the retreating car, then suddenly grabbed her backside and screamed.

"Yow! What the…?"

"What's wrong?" asked Bertie, watching Della hop in circles.

"I think a bee stung me!"

Confused, Bertie stared at her friend. Then realization dawned. "Della, did you try to use your powers to get a bee to sting that guy?

"I sure did. It was the first thing I thought of. I asked that he be stung right on the ass. Did I do it wrong? Or does that bee have no sense of direction? What happened?" Her rear end smarted, and she rubbed at it.

Bertie tried to hold back a laugh.

"What are you laughing about?" Della demanded with a scowl.

"Well, aside from you rubbing your butt in the middle of the street…?"

Della's narrowed her eyes.

"You forgot, didn't you?" asked Bertie, waving her finger.

"Forgot what?"

"How the power works. This is actually good because we just learned another thing about it. We already know that if we try to manifest something that won't serve the greater good, the powers don't work. But you took it a step further. You lost your temper and tried to do real harm to someone. It was intentional, and it backfired! Talk about instant karma. The harm you wished on that driver came back and literally bit you in the ass!" Bertie dissolved into laughter.

"Oh, great—instant karma," Della muttered. "But what about *his* karma? He nearly ran us over!"

"I think his karma is not our business," Bertie said quietly.

Della sighed. "I get it. I don't like it, but I get it. I almost imagined setting his hair on fire. Thank God I didn't try that!"

"These powers are no joke," Bertie said seriously.

"True, but they'll keep us honest, won't they. The rules force us to be less reactive. More loving."

"And if loving emotions raise our frequency, then this sounds like a decent path to help lift our consciousness."

"I hope you're right, but this is going to be a challenge for me." Della admitted. "You know my temper."

"Yeah, you and your temper are just going to have to chill. And I'm sure you will, but it will be a challenge for all of us."

"I'm not red-headed for nothing, you know." Della grinned. "It's exciting, though, don't you think? Everything's about to change."

"Oh yes, it will. And speaking of exciting, let's get a move on. The Bookies will be waiting, and they are all riled up about Cathy's clean bill of health."

"It's unbelievable, isn't it?"

Della was quiet for a moment and looked at her friend. "Hey, are you thinking what I'm thinking?"

"Oh, who knows what goes on in that head of yours?" Bertie laughed. "But what I'm thinking about is this—I'm wondering if we should give the powers to the Bookies."

"We? Do you think I can give powers to people, too?"

"I don't see why not. But should we?"

Della's face lit up. "Heck yes, we should! Let's spread this stuff around. If all we can do is good, then the faster we spread it, the better. Shoot, I wish I had given the driver in the car the powers now, instead of trying to sting him."

"Good point," Bertie said, smiling. "And I think you're right, Della. I'm so glad I shared the gift with you. I think now it's what we're supposed to be doing, and I'm learning from the sharing. Let's get to the coffee shop. I want to see the looks on the Bookies' faces when we tell them."

Della rubbed her sore rear end and said. "Just don't ask me to sit down."

"You can manifest standing up today," laughed Bertie.

CHAPTER 13

When Bertie and Della got to the cafe, the Bookies were already there, buzzing with excitement over Cathy's clean bill of health. They kept hugging her like she'd won the lottery, which was sort of the case.

"Can you believe it?" asked Cathy. "I keep telling Sue that I've never won anything in my life, and now I get this!"

Bertie gave her a big hug, her heart full. Della leaned over and whispered, "Well, go on. Tell them."

"Tell us what?" asked Bonnie.

"OK, here goes," Bertie said, rising to her feet. "Bookies, this news about Cathy is astonishing. It's the best thing that could happen. I'm so happy about this news. But listen, I've got some news for you too, but let's go back to our private room, shall we?"

The women exchanged curious glances as they followed her.

"What's going on, Bertie?" asked Sue.

"I'll bet it's good news," smiled Cathy. "This is a lucky day."

Bertie hesitated, unsure where to start, when Della jumped in.

"It's fantastic news," she blurted. "Bertie inherited superpowers from her aunt, and now I've got them too. And we're gonna give them to you!"

"Subtle, Della," muttered Bertie.

The Bookies looked at each other.

Bonnie raised her eyebrows "Oh dear. Della has finally flipped out."

"Della's always flipped out," said Bertie. "But this time? She's not wrong." She knew it would be hard to convince them, but she plowed ahead with the story. She told them everything—Aunt Maddie, the letter, the gift, and the consicouness-raising goals.

Della looked hopeful. "Isn't it amazing?" She looked around at her friends' stunned faces and added dejectedly, "Well, I have to admit that I'm a little disappointed at your reaction. I thought you'd be over the moon."

Cathy cleared her throat, "I think I speak for the rest of us, but I'm not sure what kind of joke you two are playing today. Is it supposed to be funny? Because I just don't get it."

The other Bookies nodded in agreement.

"Yeah, what gives?" asked Sue. "Why did you pick today to do silly jokes when Cathy has such amazing good news?"

Della shrugged at Bertie, "You'll just have to show them, Bertie."

"I think you're right," answered Bertie. "Okay, girls, who wants coffee?"

Sue rolled her eyes. "We can get coffee later." She was a little upset and got up to leave, fishing around in her pocket for her keys.

Then she blinked and looked down at her hand. Instead of her key ring, she now held a steaming mug of coffee.

"What the heck!" yelled Sue, nearly spilling her drink.

More mugs of coffee appeared on the table in front of each Bookie.

"How did you do that?" whispered Cathy.

"She told you," said Della, firmly. "She has powers. Do you believe her now?"

"I believe something. I'm just not sure what," said Bonnie, gaping in shock.

"Show them again, Bertie," Della urged.

"You do it this time," said Bertie. "Then they'll see. And don't go overboard, Della. I've got customers in the next room."

Della looked around and spotted a small bouquet of fresh flowers on the table. "This will be fun." She focused and the flowers doubled in size.

"What the…?" gasped Cathy.

"Keep watching," said Della. The flowers rose from the vase and floated slowly to the ceiling, growing larger all the time, then began dancing in time to the soft music played for the coffeehouse patrons.

"Good one, Della," said Bertie, clapping.

The Bookies stared, stunned.

"I think I believe you," Sue said slowly.

"Unless you've been moonlighting as a magician, I believe you too," said Cathy, wide-eyed.

Bonnie nodded then asked, "But Bertie, why you? Why were you chosen?"

"I don't actually know." Bertie admitted. "Neither did Aunt Maddie. But she said I was the one to share it and use it for good. And I believe that."

"So that's why you gave them to Della?"

Before Bertie could answer, Cathy's eyes widened. "Wait, did you two use the powers to heal me?"

Della said, "I didn't have any powers then, but I think Bertie had something to do with it."

"You saved me, Bertie," cried Cathy. "Thank you! Thank you so much!"

"I'm not sure if it was just me. Honestly? I think we all did it, but I think I helped. I believe healing is one of the powers included in the gift. That's another thing I just learned."

Sue leaned in and asked what they were all thinking, "Does this mean that you're going to give the powers to us too?"

"Yes," answered Bertie, seriously. "If you want them."

The Bookies looked at each other. Sue grinned and said excitedly, "We'd be crazy not to."

"I want to join you in this," said Cathy. "I think it's the beginning of something extraordinary, and I sure want to be part of it."

"So do I, " echoed both Sue and Bonnie. "Count us in."

"Okay then, let's do it. Della, want to try your hand at sharing the powers?"

"Sure! How do I do it?"

"Just like the flowers. Picture it. Imagine the girls receiving the powers. It's all about intention."

Della stood up straight, relaxed, and closed her eyes.. She pictured all three of the Bookies receiving and bringing their new powers out to the world. After a minute, she said softly, "Okay, I think that did it."

"That was it?" asked Cathy. "Are you sure? I didn't feel anything."

"Me neither," said Bonnie.

"Well, let me give it a try," said Sue gamely. She closed her eyes and held out her closed hand. When she opened it, a beautiful white butterfly flew out and fluttered around the room.

Sue squealed, "Della, it worked! We are now the Super Bookies!"

They all laughed, and Bertie could see that they actually glowed with excitement.

Just then, a man wearing an apron poked his head in. "Boss, come quick! The water heater's leaking all over the back room!"

Bertie jumped to her feet. "Well, shoot!" she said. "Call the plumber, and tell him it's an emergency," She turned to the others, "Della, stay with them. Help them practice their gift. I'll be back as soon as I can."

CHAPTER 14

A half-hour later, after the plumber had arrived, Bertie left him working on the water heater and hurried back to the Bookies. As she walked through the kitchen, she noticed something strange—while the broken water heater inconvenienced her, she was not that upset. Something like this would have sent her into a tailspin before. Now? It just felt like one of life's little hiccups. Calm acceptance apparently was yet unexpected gift from the powers.

Turning the corner, she called out, "The plumber's here, thank God. And we've got a lot of the mess cleaned up. How's it going in—"

She stopped dead in her tracks.

Spider webs draped from the ceiling in large swoops like Halloween gone wild. They covered the table, chairs, and even the Bookies. Not only that, standing in front and center was Bonnie, dressed in a full, polka-dotted, knitted clown costume, complete with makeup and a giant red nose.

"What the...?" muttered Bertie.

Everyone stood frozen in disbelief—except Della, who was doubled over laughing.

"Was I gone that long?" asked Bertie

"I can't stop laughing," gasped Della between giggles. "I can't breathe!"

"You wouldn't believe what happened," Cathy began.

"Try me," said Bertie, eyeing the chaos. Then it hit her. "Wait. Let me guess. Della, you forgot to tell them, didn't you?"

"I sure did!" Della wheezed, wiping tears from her eyes.

Bertie sighed. "Alright, Bookies. Here's the deal. There are a few rules surrounding the powers that we've learned. One, if you try to manifest something that will ultimately cause harm, the powers won't work. Two, if you try to cause harm on purpose, it will backfire. Big time. They are to be used to promote human consciousness. I believe that if you stick to manifesting joy, beauty, gratitude, healing, kindness, and love, you will be safe. There are probably more rules, but this is what we know so far."

"Makes sense," said Cathy, brushing away spider webs.

"What exactly did you try to manifest?" asked Bertie. "I can only imagine."

Sue raised her hand sheepishly. "I couldn't help myself," said Sue. "You know how I feel about spiders. Well, I saw one up in the corner there." She pointed.

"He won't hurt anyone," said Bertie. "They help keep the mosquitoes down in the summer."

"I know all that," Sue said miserably, shivering as she brushed away the webs from her arms. "But I panicked. So, I tried to unalive it."

"Let's call this the 'Do No Harm' rule," said Della.

"Good lesson for us all," Bertie added.

She turned to Bonnie in the clown's suit. "I give up. I can't even imagine what happened to you."

Bonnie looked sheepish. "Well, shoot. I saw Gloria Beecham out in the cafe flirting with Bert London like she didn't know he was married to Ginny. And honestly? Her makeup looked downright clownish. I just thought, if she's gonna act like that, maybe she should look the part."

"Oh, got it," said Bertie. "So, you accidentally clowned yourself."

"I guess Gloria's bad decisions are not my business," Bonnie muttered, cheeks burning.

"Well, thankfully, no one got hurt," said Bertie. "We can clean this up fast."

"Let's remember, the goal is always to be manifesting consciousness raising. We start with us, and the more we raise our own, the better we'll be at sharing the gift," said Della.

"That's right," agreed Bertie. "I've been looking into it, and there are so many ways to work on this, such as meditating, being alone and appreciating nature, kindness to others, gratitude, and breath work, to name a few. We should all be practicing these as we spread the gift around."

"Let's commit to that," said Della. "And let's check in with each other in a few days. We all need to keep in touch right now. Can y'all do a Zoom meeting on Thursday?"

The Bookies nodded and agreed on a meeting time.

"And when we start passing along the gift," Cathy added, giving Della a side-eye, "Maybe we should go over the rules first with the recipients?"

"Absolutely," agreed Bertie.

"Just tell them everything you know," said Della.

"We should put together a brochure stating the rules," suggested Bonnie.

"Good idea," said Sue.

Bertie added, "You know, if this is as big as I think it will be, we need to get the media involved. How do we get the word out?"

"I've got a cousin at the TV station in Baton Rouge, and Bonnie's sister works on radio," suggested Sue.

"I know a reporter with the newspaper," added Cathy.

"And I can build us a website and launch some social media," said Della.

"Wow, you Bookies make an amazing team," said Bertie, beaming.

"Let's get to work," said Cathy. "We should start right here and now at the coffeehouse. Bertie, you tell your staff. Show them your pot-stirring trick. I'll go talk to the customers out front. Maybe grow some flowers. Don't forget to tell them the rules. Sue and Cathy, can you clean up the mess in here?"

Della giggled. "Bonnie, you should probably just go change. I doubt your clown couture is going to inspire trust. But you can tell your knitting group later."

"Alright, then. Let's spread the word and stay in touch. Meanwhile, everyone should read as much as possible about consciousness, OK?" said Bertie.

"On it!" the Bookies chorused, energized and glowing.

CHAPTER 15

"Is everyone here?" asked Bertie, smiling on the Zoom call.

"Hey, y'all!" came back a chorus of cheerful Bookie greetings.

"Great. Let's check in on how things are going with the powers. Della, how about you go first?"

"Right," said Della. "Well, I've been sharing this gift nonstop. Our website is now live, and we've got Facebook, Instagram, and TikTok up and running. I texted y'all the links. I uploaded the rules everywhere I could. If you think of anything new people should know about the gift, let me know and I'll add it in right away. People are clamoring for information already. Bertie, how about sharing the letter from your Aunt Maddie on the website to give a little background?"

"Great idea, Della. Okay, how about you, Sue?"

"I've been sharing a lot too, and I printed leaflets spelling out the rules. I'll drop some off at the Bump and Grind, so you can all make copies. Also, I've been meditating out in the woods near the horse ranch. I've always loved being out in nature, but now? It's like the trees are sending out a special energy to me. I come out buzzing! Y'all need to try this."

"Share that with people, Sue. Maybe give Della a quote for the website about it. I can't wait to try it," said Cathy. "I've been meditating too, with music. The right songs put me in a great headspace instantly. I recommend putting something about that on the website."

Bonnie chimed in, "I'm sharing the gift, too. My knitting group has added a meditation practice to our meetings, just like the Bookies. And I'm practicing gratitude every day. I'm finding that you can't be in a state of gratitude and a state of fear or anger at the same time. It helps me feel joy and grateful for everyone's presence and being. I swear, even going to the grocery store feels magical now. I found myself dancing along to the piped-in music in the produce aisle the other day. I shared the gift with other shoppers, and they were all glowing from the powers—and happiness!"

"I love that," Bertie said. "And I'm meditating too. It's become my favorite time of day. I've read that meditating physically rewires the brain, less stress and more focus and creativity. Let's emphasize this on the website and socials, Della, okay?"

"Absolutely," Della said. "Keep sending me stories and ideas. People are hungry for this."

"OK, let's meet in person soon," Bertie said. "Now that we're all in this together, I can't see enough of y'all!"

CHAPTER 16

Two months later.

Synthra Lewis had just hung up the phone when her assistant, Lindy, poked her head through the office door at Neurosea Inc.

"Got a minute?" she asked.

"You of all people know I don't," Synthra grunted, scrolling on her phone.

"I really only need half a minute," Lindy said, crossing the room with her laptop. "I have to show you something important—and troubling."

She set the laptop down in front of Synthra and pointed to a graph.

"What am I looking at?" she asked, not hiding her impatience.

"As you know, we can track *Mirajubil* sales in many ways, including geographically. This graph shows New Orleans."

"Yes, and…?"

"Normally, the sales trend upward worldwide. But look here."

Synthra squinted. The bar graph showed a sharp decline in *Mirajubil* sales over the last two months in just one demographic area, New Orleans.

"Is this some kind of mistake?" Synthra snapped, snatching the laptop.

"There's no mistake. We're hemorrhaging customers in that market."

"Is it Mardi Gras season or something? " Synthra offered, trying to sound light. "Maybe folks are too busy partying to be depressed."

She was only half-joking, but she was alarmed. Her eyes never left the screen.

"No, it's not. I don't have an explanation, but I knew you'd want to know."

Synthra narrowed her eyes. "You like your job, don't you, Lindy?"

Lindy stiffened. "Yes, I do. Very much."

Synthra's thoughts were furious, *"Then find out what the hell is happening in New Orleans, and fast, if you want to keep it."*

But she simply hissed, "Get back to me when you find the cause."

"Right, boss," answered Lindy shakily, then grabbed her laptop and fled the office.

CHAPTER 17

Two days later, Lindy once again knocked and entered Synthra's office. "I found something, and you're not going to like it."

Synthra looked up from her computer screen. "What are you jabbering about?"

"Our New Orleans market, remember?" she prompted, setting her laptop on Synthra's desk and turning the screen towards her boss, with split screens showing two graphs. "Here's *Mirajubil* sales in New Orleans—still dropping. And now here's something interesting. This other graph shows crime rates and traffic accidents dropping too."

Synthra studied the screen carefully. "What in the world is going on down there?"

"I think I found something," Lindy said, and clicked to a news website playing a video from WBRV TV in Baton Rouge. The screen showed a chipper blond reporter on the street in front of a coffeehouse holding a microphone and waiting for a cue.

"This is Susan Skoog with WBRV coming to you this morning from the Bump and Grind Coffeehouse in New Orleans. We're here to ask the question on everyone's mind—what is going on in the Big Easy? Our sources say something remarkable is happening. Crime, violence, and even automobile accidents are down, and people are, well, happier—of all things!" She made an ironic gesture for the camera.

"We're here with Bertie Ryan, owner of the Bump and Grind Coffeehouse. Bertie, everyone I've spoken to in town about this phenomenon told me I should interview you. They say that you are the founder of this happiness movement, if that's what you want to call it."

Cut to Bertie, smiling at the camera. "Oh my. Well, I'm far from the founder. We don't know for sure who the founder is because this movement goes way back, handed down from generations, but I feel positive that you can give Source the credit. Some people would call him God." She said with a twinkle in her eye.

The reporter hesitated and then asked, "God? Is that so?" She held up a local newspaper to the camera and said, "This article is titled 'New Orleans is SAFE!' and cites crime statistics. It also mentions you, Ms. Ryan. So, what's really going on? Fill us in."

Bertie chuckled and said, "I'll tell you what. Consider this an invitation to you and your photographer, and anyone who's listening out there, to come to a meeting we have planned for today. If you want to see what is happening in the city, then come and see for yourselves. I promise it will be worth your while. And yes, New Orleans is safer, and we'll show you why at the meeting. Be at the City Park Peristyle at one PM tomorrow. If you want answers, be there!"

Bertie waved goodbye, and the reporter signed off dramatically with, "You heard it here, folks. The Big Easy is living up to its name. We'll report to you live at one PM tomorrow. Stay tuned to WBRV TV for the whole story." Then she immediately got on the phone with her editor. She wasn't going to miss that meeting.

Bertie walked back into the Bump and Grind, and Della was waiting for her. "The media is showing up! It's happening, girlfriend."

⌒

After watching the video, Synthra slammed the laptop shut. She didn't want to panic, but a drop in sales in a major market like New Orleans was enough to worry her. If something like this happened in more cities, the company could be in trouble, and her job could be at risk. She glared at Lindy.

"I don't know what this is, but I'm about to find out. Get me on a plane to New Orleans first thing tomorrow. And get me Governor Bushy in Baton Rouge on the line. He's not going to like this one bit."

The governor, a major Louisiana stockholder in Neurosea, Inc., and an acquaintance of Synthra's, picked up immediately.

Synthra jumped right in. "Governor Bushey, what is going on in New Orleans? *Mirajubil* sales have tanked. Crime's down. People are happy. I mean, what the hell?" She told him about the tracked drop in sales of the antidepressant. "And now the media is sniffing around the story, even the Baton Rouge TV stations, so the same thing could happen there. We need to get on top of this. I don't have to tell you how this will hit your pocketbook as well as ours."

"Synthra, you were right to call me," said the governor.

Synthra went on. "I'm heading down to New Orleans in the morning. We've got to stop these people. I'm talking specifically about this woman, Bertie Ryan, who owns the Bump and Grind Coffeehouse. I think we're dealing with a cult here, and you can't have that in your state, right? Normally, I wouldn't give a hoot about it, but this one is picking our pockets. You need to fix this now." She promised to check in the next day and signed off.

Governor Bushey leaned his corpulent body back in his leather chair and focused his beady brown eyes on the Mississippi River slithering through Baton Rouge. He was the worst kind of old-school politician—oily, corrupt, and charm-coated. His wife drove a new car every year, and he and his family vacationed several times a year at the expense of kickbacks from corporations seeking favors. He was a stout, powerful man with a receding hairline and a growing list of people in his pocket across the country. One of those people was Glen Lacombe, the current Mayor of New Orleans. Mayor Lacombe owed his election win to Governor Bushey's influence and backing. The mayor was a weak man and was stuck as far in the governor's pocket as an old wallet.

The governor called him immediately. "Glen, how's the family?"

"We're all just fine down here, Governor. Good to hear from you." Inside his meticulously neat office, the mayor stood at attention in his natty suit, bowtie, and shoes while talking to Governor Bushey. He had been waiting to hear from the governor since his election. He owed his political career to Bushey, and he was grateful. Lacombe enjoyed being mayor; it was a job with many perks. He knew payback day would come, and here it was. Whatever the governor wanted was a done deal.

"I need a favor," said the Governor.

"Of course. What can I do for you?"

"There is a certain cafe in your city—the Bump and Grind."

"Yes, I know that place. I even dropped by there one day. The name makes it sound like it should be on Bourbon Street," laughed the mayor.

"Well, Glen, I've heard some disturbing things about it. Word is, a dangerous cult is operating out of it."

"No kidding," said the mayor. "That's a new one. What proof do we have?"

The Governor slitted his eyes, thinking, "*You don't need proof, you pissant.*" He went on smoothly, "Glen, trust me on this. That place is not only dangerous, I hear it has several violations that would interest the Health Department, if you know what I mean?"

Realization dawned on the Mayor. "Oh, I see."

"Yes," the Governor went on, "I think the Health Department needs to look into those violations right away."

Mayor Lacombe took a deep breath. "First thing tomorrow morning, okay?"

"That's fine. And call the press. Make it look like you're cleaning up the city. Be there yourself—take credit."

"OK, Governor. Consider it done."

"See that it is, Mayor," said the Governor, and hung up.

CHAPTER 18

t nine AM the following morning, Health Department Inspector Bob Gleason stood at the front door of the Bump and Grind. The word had come down from his boss that the media might show up here, so he had dressed the part: perfectly pressed chinos, starched, white shirt, navy blue tie with gold clasp, and his badge shining like a warning light. He tried to hand Bertie a handful of inspection paperwork.

Bertie glanced at the papers. "Mr. Gleason, what is this about? We weren't scheduled for any inspection today."

"You may call me Health Inspector Gleason, Ms. Ryan," he replied icily. "And the Health Department does not need to schedule inspections. Today's surprise inspection proves why this is a good policy. We found numerous serious violations."

Outside, a small crowd gathered. WNOW TV from New Orleans and WBRV from Baton Rouge were unloading equipment. A reporter from the local newspaper hovered nearby.

"What are you talking about?" Bertie asked, frowning.

"We received a tip that this place was in a dangerous condition. "

"Show me," Bertie challenged. "Where are all those violations, Inspector? My crew cleans this place like it was their own home. Shoot, I help clean it myself."

Gleason read from his clipboard. "Rodent droppings. Leaking pipe. Refrigerator temp off. Food labels missing. Unsafe cleaning practices. Hairnet violations, Improper utensil storage. Shall I go on?"

"You and I both know this is fiction. Why are you really here?"

Before he could answer, out on the street, Mayor Lacombe stepped out of his black limousine and strode confidently up to an already assembled microphone. Bertie opened the front door to hear what he was saying to the press.

Standing proudly at his full five-foot-five height, the Mayor bellowed, "My office has been informed that this establishment not only violates health codes but is the headquarters of a dangerous cult as well. Its leader is Bertie Ryan, owner of the Bump and Grind Coffeehouse. There's Ms. Ryan now." He pointed in Bertie's direction, and the press immediately swarmed in her directions and questions flew.

"Is it true, Ms. Ryan? Are you running a cult?"

"Is it true that the Bump and Grind is violating health codes? Shoot, I eat here!"

"Any comments on the accusations?"

"Whoa," laughed Bertie. "Okay, people, let me clear this up. There's a misunderstanding here. There are no health code violations at the Bump and Grind. My place is clean as a whistle. Come in and see for yourselves!"

She went on, "And as far as any cult allegations, well, I'm not sure where the mayor got that notion from, but…" She thought a moment, and a smile snuck onto her face. "Let me just repeat the invitation I made yesterday. If you want to know the truth about what's going on in the Bump and Grind, in New Orleans, and all over the place - and what all this cult and health department nonsense is all about—and believe me, the truth is fascinating—you can all find out everything you need to know this afternoon at the Peristyle in City Park at one o'clock. All of you are invited, including everyone watching this on TV." She looked right into the TV cameras, "Come on out later today, and we will clear all this up once and for all. Everyone's invited—even you, Mayor Lacombe!"

She thanked the media crews and hurried back inside to Health Inspector Gleason. He again extended the inspection papers.

"I'm authorized to tell you," he said ominously, "Shut down your cult, or I can shut down your cafe."

Bertie looked him in the eye. "Alright, I see what this is." She placed a gentle hand on the man's shoulder. "Okay, here's what I'm going to do. I'm giving you a gift today, Inspector. And then you can keep your bogus papers."

"I can't accept any gifts. Are you trying to bribe me?"

"Nothing of the sort," answered Bertie with a smile. She then envisioned the inspector attending the City Park gathering that afternoon, full of light and truth.

"I'll see you at the park," she said with a smile, and handed him one of their new printouts with the rules of the gift. "Read this, and have a great day."

———⌒———

Synthra texted the Governor shortly after landing in New Orleans.

"Just caught the press conference about the Bump and Grind with Mayor Lacombe. Health inspection was a stroke of genius. Headed to City Park now. I'll be sure to meet Bertie Ryan and keep pressure on the mayor. "

His reply was only three words, "Get it done."

CHAPTER 19

At one o'clock, Bertie and the Bookies looked out at the sea of faces surrounding the City Park Peristyle. Many were regulars from the Bump and Grind who had already received the gift. Others were curious onlookers drawn by the press. And, of course, there was the press itself.

Bertie had no microphone, which concerned her until Mayor Lacombe's crew arrived to set one up for him. Apparently, he planned to speak to the crowd that afternoon as well.

Della and the Bookies exchanged nervous glances. They expected another public attack. Quietly, they visualized a shield of protection around Bertie. Della marveled at her friend. Bertie looked calm in the middle of this potential maelstrom and even greeted the mayor, shaking his hand and chatting with him, smiling. And was he smiling back at her?

Synthra pulled up in an Uber and hurried to the front of the crowd. She was relieved to see Mayor Lacombe already on stage. She would connect with him afterwards. Between the two of them, they needed to corral this "cult of happiness" before it did any more corporate damage.

TV and newspaper crews jockeyed for the best shot. Susan Skoog from WBRV TV in Baton Rouge was front and center, feeling something electric in the air. Her reporter's instincts tingled.

Then the mayor tapped the mic and began.

Synthra watched him with a smile. *"Here it comes,"* she thought. *"The mayor will shut them down for good, and things will go back to our anxiety-filled norm."*

The mayor began, sounding like the smooth politician he was. "Friends, I can't tell you how happy I am that so many of you came out this afternoon. When there's something wrong with our city, I must address it. We all must address it."

Synthra was grinning now. *"He's going to out them as a cult and maybe even shut down that coffeehouse. It sure is good to have friends in high places."* She focused in on the mayor's words.

"This morning, I gave a press conference about a supposed cult at the Bump and Grind Coffeehouse and a pending health department shutdown. I'm here to correct those misunderstandings."

"You tell 'em!" thought Synthra. Then her eyes widened and she said out loud, "Wait, what?"

"That's right," the mayor went on. "The health department shutdown of the Bump and Grind was misinformation. They passed their inspection with flying colors."

The crowd murmured in surprise.

He continued with a smile, "And those dangerous cult rumors? Just ridiculous. All false. There is no cult."

Synthra gulped and started to sweat. *"What is this fool doing? The Governor will squash his little mayoral butt. And the board of Neurosea will squash mine if we don't shut this down right here and now."*

The Mayor continued, "Ms. Bertie Ryan, owner of the Bump and Grind, is here to share what's really happening in our city. I'm honored to hand over this mic to her right now."

He passed it to Bertie, who stepped forward, surrounded by the Bookies. She looked directly into the TV cameras. "Hi, everyone," she said warmly. "I'm Bertie Ryan, and I own the spotlessly clean Bump and Grind Coffeehouse." The crowd chuckled. "I don't need to tell you that these are strange times. We are divided, and anxious, and searching for answers. So, I'm just here to tell you that our city is changing, and the world is changing—and it's about time, don't you think? It's our time. Time to become who we really are: happy, fulfilled, and powerful."

Synthra could stand it no longer. She ran up the steps and grabbed the microphone from Bertie. "People, don't listen to her!" she shouted, "This is a cult! She's going to tell you things that aren't true because she wants you to join them. You and I know that people aren't meant to be all la-di-da and happy all the time. That's impossible. Life is hard, and we are human. We have to be careful, suspicious, and watch out for ourselves. Protect yourself! There's always someone out there who will take advantage of you. To hurt you. Don't listen. I'm Synthra Lewis, CEO of Neurosea Inc. I represent science, not this mumbo-jumbo. You want happiness? Trust doctors. Trust science. We have medicine, and it works."

The crowd stared. Synthra panted under the weight of the moment and the scorching afternoon sun. She felt panic and the closeness of the crowd. She started to sway and put her hand out for help.

"Synthra," said Bertie, gently taking her hand. "You look like you're about to faint." She turned to Della, "We have some cold water, don't we?"

Della hurried to grab a bottle from a nearby ice chest, and Synthra took a sip, still breathless.

Bertie continued, watching the other woman, "Synthra, I have something special for you."

"Yeah, yeah. Thanks for the water," said Synthra, muttering.

Bertie smiled, then closed her eyes and whispered, "I'm picturing you happy, doing good for people—your clients, your employees, and yes, even the governor. That's right. The mayor told me who you are and your connection with the governor. So, I'm envisioning you and the mayor in charge of paying a little visit to the governor to share your new gift."

Bertie opened her eyes and watched a faint glow light up Synthra's expression.

Synthra blinked, visibly stunned. She stared at Bertie and felt a burden leave her heart. Something inside her shifted. After a moment, she looked around at the crowd and said slowly into the mic, "It's okay, everybody. I'm alright now."

The crowd broke into applause.

She turned to the mic one last time. "Mayor Lacombe, I need a minute of your time. May I have a word?" He waved her over to the side of the stage.

Then she stepped away but not before saying, "Listen to this lady, folks. Bertie Ryan is onto something."

With the mic returned to her, Bertie turned back to the crowd. "There's a lot of work to be done, so I'll keep this short." She signaled to the Bookies, who began handing out sheets of paper to everyone in the crowd, then continued, "We have something for you today." And with that, Bertie gave the gift to everyone in the audience. She turned to the TV cameras and said, "And if you're watching from home, this gift is for you too."

And with that, Bertie sent the gift out into the world. She paused, feeling something rise in the air.

She told the crowd, "You are going to feel different from now on. The world has been waiting for us to change, and now is the time. Right now. Can you feel it happening already? You're already brighter, lighter."

The crowd murmured. People looked around and felt themselves smiling. Those who were sick felt better. The colors in the park, sky, and even in their neighbors' faces looked brighter. There was a glow. Suspicions gave way to a sense of kinship. For the first time in a long time, they felt happier.

Bertie continued, "You want to know what's happening in this city? It's the same as what's happening in the world. And now you're a part of it. You've been given a gift—or powers—that are supposed to help raise our consciousness. They can't buy yachts, wealth, or revenge. They bring love. And we're here to spread it. You're going to hear a lot about this in the coming weeks. It's an experience that will grow, and the more it grows, the stronger it gets. Just as I gave you the gift, now you can give this gift to others—in person, by phone, video, and social media. And you must share it. Because this is our purpose. We are here to raise the collective human consciousness. And listen, this is important and will save you a lot of trouble. My friends are handing out flyers that explain a bit about this gift. It tells you where it came from, how to make it work, and, just as important, what not to do, which we discovered the hard way. It comes with rules, so read the sheet, okay?" She stopped and smiled at her friends in the crowd. All of the Bookies were happily handing out flyers. Bonnie handed out knitted potholders along with her papers.

Bertie held up one of the flyers. "We can use this gift to manifest a better world. And that, in case you were wondering, is what we are supposed to do here on earth. It starts with us, and it works just by working to raise your own consciousness and sharing the gift. It's the most important thing in the world that you can do. There's a website on the sheet that you can visit and learn more. Use it and share it."

She looked out at the sea of glowing faces.

"That's it. You've got a job to do now. We all do. And it's the best job that ever was. As for me, I'll keep sharing the gift every chance I have. Meanwhile, if any of you need me, I'll be serving coffee at the Bump and Grind. Come by and see us sometime!"

She stepped offstage into the arms of the Bookies, Della grabbed her and whispered, "Bertie Ryan, you just saved the freakin' world!"

CHAPTER 20

Synthra got the Governor on the phone from the mayor's limousine. "Governor Bushey, I'm here with Mayor Lacombe. Did you catch the TV broadcast of the New Orleans meeting with that Ryan woman?"

"No," the governor replied. "I've been in meetings all morning. Update me."

"We will—face to face. Mayor Lacombe and I are driving to Baton Rouge in his car right now."

"Now?" said the governor, surprised.

"Yes, sir, that's right. We have important news, and you're going to want to hear about it firsthand."

She ended the call, turned to the mayor with a grin and grabbed his arm, "C'mon, Mayor, let's go give the governor a present."

CHAPTER 21

The following morning, the Bookies gathered at the Bump and Grind to watch the national news. Susan Skoog of WBRV TV's broadcast was replaying from the day before at City Park. Then, the segment cut to a growing map of states reporting instances of people receiving a strange power—and a glow. The gift was spreading so quickly, it was almost impossible to track.

The Bookies sensed yet another change in energy as the country watched, and the powers spread through the media. The energy was stronger, calmer, more electric.

By midday, news stations across the globe were picking up the story. Translations appeared in dozens of languages. The Bookies felt a further shift. The world's energy held a mix of peaceful awe and a sense of possibility none of them had ever felt before.

Cathy leaned forward, eyes wide, "The more the gift spreads, the stronger it becomes. It seems to take effect on people immediately now, whereas it took a little while to work on us when we first started."

Bertie nodded. "It also feels like the gift has taken on a life of its own at this point. People aren't just sharing it anymore—it's moving on its own. You know, I think people could always manifest these powers, they just didn't know and believe that they could."

Della nodded. "They just needed a spark. Someone to remind them who we really are." She turned and whispered to Bertie with a grin, "You did it, Bertie. And to think I knew you when you were just my crazy friend."

Bertie grinned back, "We all did it, Della. And we've only just begun. There's more to come—more growth, higher frequencies, deeper connections. Life will be better. Humans will be better. We'll probably still screw up now and then, but we know better now. And our lives will be richer, more open to experiences we've only dreamed of."

"I'm happy just to be here now," said Della, full of wonder.

"Yes," smiled Bertie. "And maybe that's the whole point."

CHAPTER 22

That afternoon, a letter arrived at Bertie's house from Attorney Michael Gray. Inside was an envelope with a bold number "4" written on it, along with a note that read:

Dear Ms. Ryan:

Your aunt gave me this final letter for you with strict instructions not to deliver it until "the time was right." When I inquired when that time might be, Maddie said, "You'll know, Michael."

As vague and maddening as that was, we were dear friends, and I trusted her, and I was determined to fulfill my duties.

I believe from watching you on the news that, without a doubt, this is the time.

Keep up the good work.

Warmly,
Michael Gray

Bertie's hands trembled a little as she opened the envelope. Her heart ached with love as she read these words in her aunt's familiar handwriting:

Dear Bertie,

Well, isn't this just a kick in the head? I know you are experiencing an actual change in human evolution. I just wish I could be there to watch it unfold. But something tells me, maybe I am!

Humans are so much more than we have convinced ourselves that we are. With your help, we're waking up and realizing that we are all connected and need to help each other. And with that realization, we will begin making new choices now.. We will start to revere life and our planet.

We needed a shift in consciousness to survive. Separation was killing us. But knowing that we are all one? Well, that's what will heal us. Our true identity is awareness. Our purpose is to rise into that awareness, to become our higher selves.

People need to remember that when life disturbs them, they simply need to step back and see it through the eyes of their higher selves and ask themselves—does this bring me joy? Does it align with the universe? It's so simple, but we lost our way for centuries.

With God's help, you, my dear, as well as all of us, will restore it. We just needed a little nudge. And a swift kick in the ass!

Man, I'm proud of you—and I'm not even alive! Hehe.

Stay the path, dear Bertie. I'm loving you from wherever I am!

Aunt Maddie

Bertie sat on the edge of her sofa, the letter trembling slightly in her hands. She read the last line again. *"Man, I'm proud of you—and I'm not even alive!"* She felt something warm open up in her heart. Tears streamed down her cheeks, soft and steady, like a long-awaited summer rain. The world went quiet around her, as if even the universe paused to listen.

She pressed the letter to her heart and whispered, "Thank you, Aunt Maddie. Thank you for believing in me when I couldn't see what was coming. Thank you for this gift—for this chance to see the world with open eyes."

Her voice cracked as she added, "Thank you, God, for choosing me."

The full weight of the journey—the miracles, the fears, the laughter, the mystery—washed over her. And in that moment, she felt the truth of it all. This mattered. Not just because people were smiling more or feeling connected. Not because crime had dropped or flowers danced in midair. But because something sacred was being restored—a sacred dance with the infinite. Something nearly lost to time.

Bathed in golden light, she whispered to the stillness, "I will not waste this. I will share it until my last breath. I will give and give and give again. I get it now. I finally get it."

EPILOGUE

I f Earth were seen from above, starting with a simple bird's-eye view of the Bump and Grind, and slowly zoomed out, the planet would appear…transformed.

At the Bump and Grind, Della played the piano, and the Bookies broke out into a happy dance as more reports kept coming in about the gift spreading.

In Natchez, Aunt Maddie's neighbors and friends, Shirley, Sharon, and Attorney Michael Grey, watched the news, received the gift, and thought to themselves, "Oh, Maddie. Now it all makes sense."

After sharing the gift with the Louisiana governor, Synthra Lewis flew home to Dallas, met with her Board of Directors, and passed the gift to them. They unanimously voted to lower prices on medication and curb the aggressive marketing of antidepressants.

Strangers on the street began smiling at one another, not with politeness, but with real connection.

Farmers rethought their use of pesticides and turned toward organic crops.

Soldiers laid down their weapons, realizing that they were fighting extensions of themselves.

World leaders reached for their phones to call their global neighbors for long-overdue chats—not to posture, but to collaborate. They planned meetings on clean energy, plastic usage, healthcare, and ocean restoration, asking one collective question: "In the time we have left, what good can we do together?"

In open fields, mountain tops, and auditoriums, large groups of meditators gathered to envision the world's enlightenment.

Humankind began to thrive, not just barely survive.

From space, Earth shimmered with golden light, rippling from continent to continent, crossing borders, climbing mountains, drifting across oceans. Not a fire. Not a war. But a glow.

Something sacred had returned.

Nothing could be more beautiful.

The End.

A NOTE FROM JAX

If you're holding this book in your hands (or your lap, or awkwardly above your head in bed), I want to thank you—not just for reading, but for being someone who is curious, open-hearted, and willing to grow. Raising our consciousness isn't about floating off into the clouds or getting everything "right." It's about showing up, again and again, with more awareness, compassion, and curiosity. Some days it feels like a cosmic breakthrough; other days, it's just not yelling at the rush hour traffic.

Instead of running around trying this, that, and the other newest spiritual trend, we need to simplify, focus our efforts, and share what we know. Sprinkle your newfound awakening around like confetti. It's contagious! Sharing and working together, humans will thrive.

Please do what you can to spread the word. The world needs all of us. Use whatever gifts you have to raise human consciousness. If you're an artist, paint the message. A teacher, teach it. A writer, write it. A friend, share it. A leader, lead it. In the book I ask the question – What if one person could change the world with a single thought? I can't help but ask – what if that one person was you?

Wherever you are on your journey, keep going. The world needs your light, your questions, and your courage to evolve. We're in this together, and I'm so glad we found each other on the page. Let's keep in touch, and meanwhile, I'll be here, glitter in hand and dancing shoes on!

Recommended viewing at www.gaia.com:

Key Principles for Raising Consciousness

Awareness: Becoming more aware of your thoughts, feelings, and actions, as well as the world around you.

Intention: Setting clear intentions for your actions and aligning them with your values.

Choice: Making conscious choices about your thoughts, actions, and environment.

Acceptance: Accepting yourself and your experiences without judgment.

Gratitude: Appreciating the positive aspects of your life.

Kindness: Feeling empathy for humans and all the creatures of the earth.

Presence: Being fully present in the moment.

Positive Impact: Striving to make a positive impact on the world.

Practices for Raising Consciousness

By consistently engaging in these practices and principles, you can gradually cultivate a higher level of consciousness and experience a greater sense of well-being and connection.

Meditation:
Quieting the mind and focusing on your breath or a mantra can help you observe your thoughts and feelings without judgment, leading to greater self-awareness.

Mindfulness:
Paying attention to the present moment, without getting carried away by thoughts or emotions, can help you connect with your senses and your surroundings.

Self-Reflection:
Taking time to examine your beliefs, values, and motivations can help you understand yourself better and identify areas for growth.

Setting Intentions:
Consciously choosing your goals and how you want to show up in the world can help you align your actions with your values.

Practicing Gratitude:
Focusing on the positive aspects of your life can shift your perspective and increase your appreciation for what you have.

Conscious Breathing:
Paying attention to your breath can help you become more aware of your body and your emotions.

Mindful Movement:
Activities like yoga or Taichi can help you connect with your body and increase your awareness of your physical state.

Being Present in Nature:
Spending time outdoors and connecting with nature can help you feel more grounded and connected to the world around you.

Practicing Kindness:
When your focus is on something other than yourself and on others, you begin to realize how our lives are entangled, and, in fact, one.

HOW TO MEDITATE

It has been said that praying is talking to God/Source and meditating is listening. I like to think of it as uploading and downloading. I begin each meditation with a question for Source – "What would you have me know today?" Then I sit back and listen.

1. Find a quiet space: Choose a place where you can relax without distractions, like your bedroom or a peaceful corner.

2. Get comfortable: Sit in a chair or on the floor with a straight but relaxed spine. You can also lie down if that's more comfortable for you.

3. Close your eyes (optional): You can close your eyes to minimize visual distractions, but if it feels uncomfortable, leave them slightly open and gaze softly downwards.

4. Focus on your breath: Pay attention to the sensation of your breath as it enters and leaves your body. Notice the rise and fall of your chest or belly, or the coolness of the air entering your nostrils.

5. Return your focus: Your mind will inevitably wander. When you notice this, gently bring your attention back to your breath without judgment.

6. Be patient and kind: Meditation takes practice. Be patient with yourself, and don't get discouraged if your mind wanders frequently. Just keep bringing your attention back to your breath.

7. Start with short sessions: Begin with 5-10 minutes and gradually increase the duration as you become more comfortable.

ACKNOWLEDGMENTS

Huge thanks to my editor, Elizabeth Frey, who wielded her red pen like a Zen master with a lightsaber—merciless, precise, and somehow still full of love.

To my brave readers: thank you for making it through the weird, the wild, and the "wait…what?" moments with grace and caffeine.

And finally, to all the courageous souls out there trying to raise their consciousness every day—whether through meditation, journaling, or just resisting the urge to yell at their Wi-Fi routers— you are the real heroes. Keep going. You're doing cosmic work.

Love,
Jax

ABOUT THE AUTHOR

Jax Frey

ax Frey is a storyteller who uses both writing and painting to uplift, awaken, and connect—rooted in soulful New Orleans and blossoming into universal consciousness.

Born in New Orleans, she came into this world with a sense of celebration of culture, food, family, and fun. Translating that celebration into her writing and onto canvas is her true calling. Her colorful art depicts everything from her Rising Consciousness series, to her dancing *Gumbeaux Sistahs* paintings, and don't forget her popular line of original Mini paintings. Over 30,000 original mini paintings have been created and sold into art collections worldwide, and Jax holds a World Record for *The Most Original Acrylic Paintings on Canvas by One Artist.* Jax splits her time between New Orleans and Natchez, MS and can be found writing in her favorite local coffeehouses every day with her loveable, incorrigible pug/tornadoes, Lucy and Ethel.

Contact Jax for her available dates for book signings, Zoom meetings, and speaking engagements.

Sign up for news about her art/books at:
www.artbyjax.com
Facebook and Instagram: **Jax Frey**

ATTENTION

Please remember to recommend *Side Effects May Include Dancing*
for your next book club meeting—thanks!

Don't forget reviews!

Reviews on **Amazon.com and social media** are the biggest compliment
you can pay a writer. Please share your reading experience of Jax Frey's
novels:

- Help others make good book choices
- Help your authors get the word out about their work.

**<u>If you enjoyed the book,</u> please leave a review of your favorites on
www.amazon.com and share on Social Media. Thanks!**

OTHER BOOKS BY JAX FREY

The Gumbeaux Sistahs
(1st book in *Gumbeaux Sistahs* series)

Five fiery, Southern women wage a hilarious war against the problems of a sistah-in-trouble, using their improbable friendships, unpredictable schemes, oh-so-numerous cocktails, and a shared passion for good gumbo. *The Gumbeaux Sistahs* is a heart-warming, laugh-out-loud story you won't want to put down.

**The Gumbeaux Sistahs is an official
selection of the Pulpwood Queens,
(The largest book club in the world, with
over 800 book clubs registered.)**

Gumbeaux Love

(2nd book in the *Gumbeaux Sistahs* series)

Single, Southern artist Judith Lafferty casually confesses to her Gumbeaux Sistahs that she is occasionally lonely and would like to fall in love again. Seriously—you'd think that by now she would know to keep her mouth shut around these women. The Sistahs tackle her problem, along with their own love challenges, with their usual unreasonable, extreme plots and schemes, including a kidnapping, a cupid costume, and trying out  pick-up lines at the deli cheese counter. In helping out their friend, the Sistahs help each other as well and bring to light the many flavors of love. Be ready for twists, turns, laugh-out-loud times, and heart-wrenching moments. You'll be sure to recognize yourself and your close friends in the unstoppable sistahs.

<u>Gumbeaux Magic</u>
(3rd Book of the *Gumbeaux Sistahs* series)

Oh my gravy! What's next? You never know when life's magic spells will hit you upside the head, and the Sistahs' tribulations are just getting started. One sistah is arrested, one is widowed, another is threatened by a younger woman, and yet another is dealing with an attempted abduction! If there is one thing this group of unstoppable women is good at, it's getting together for some amazing gumbo and brainstorming the most unexpected solutions to life's difficulties.

<u>Tales of the Friendship Bench</u>
(4th Book of the *Gumbeaux Sistahs* series)

The Gumbeaux Sistahs all thought it was such a great idea to build a Friendship Bench in front of their art gallery. It was close by, and it offered a safe place and a friendly ear to visitors to talk about their lives and troubles with one sistah or another. The problem was, you never knew who was going to show up! When a thief, a pushy matriarch, a struggling artist, and a stubborn patient visit the bench, the Sistahs are overwhelmed and

go scrambling for help. But never underestimate the power of strong friendship—or of a Gumbeaux Sistah!

Crow Music
(5th Book of the *Gumbeaux Sistahs* series)

When a flock of crows starts plaguing Dawn Berard's house, she's left grappling with the bizarre mystery of their relentless visits. What could they possibly want from her, and why now? As if that weren't enough, a shocking letter arrives, addressed to her late husband, Dan, from a woman claiming to have shared a spiritual journey with him years ago—while he was married to Dawn! Stunned and curious, Dawn turns to her loyal Gumbeaux Sistahs for their trademark, no-holds-barred advice!

All Jax's novels are available at **Amazon.com**
in paperback and Kindle versions.

Sign up for news about Jax's new art/books at: <u>www.artbyjax.com</u>

CONSCIOUSNESS JOURNALING

This journal portion of the book is your companion on the journey inspired by *Side Effects May Include Dancing*—a story of women, friendship, joy, and the extraordinary power of raising consciousness. Just like the characters, you'll find space here to reflect on your own connections, awakenings, and the ways love, laughter, and community can shift your life.

Use these pages and prompts to capture insights, celebrate small miracles, and honor the friendships that lift you higher. May this journal remind you that transformation doesn't have to be solitary— it can be joyful, shared, and sometimes even involve a little dancing.

Raising Consciousness

What does *raising your consciousness* mean to you right now?

____

____

____

____

____

____

How do you notice the difference between fear-based thoughts and love-based thoughts?

What small daily ritual helps you feel more connected to your higher self?

Friendship & Connection

Who are the people in your life—the ones who lift you up no matter what?

____

____

____

____

____

____

Describe the qualities you most treasure in friendship.

____

____

____

____

____

How can you show up for your friends in ways that raise *their* consciousness, too?

Joy & Everyday Miracles

What small thing today felt like a miracle?

Write about a time you laughed until you cried. What made it so freeing?

Where in your life can you welcome more playfulness?

Love & Healing

How can you offer yourself the same kindness you offer others?

Write a love letter to yourself. What do you most need to hear?

What old wound are you ready to release, and what new gift are you ready to receive?

____

____

____

____

____

____

How does forgiveness—of yourself or others—raise your energy?

____

____

____

____

____

Vision & Manifestation

What would your life look like if you lived fully awake and conscious?

____

____

____

____

____

____

What do you most want to manifest right now? Write it as if it has already come true.

____

____

____

____

____

____

How can you use your gifts to serve the greater good?

____

____

____

____

____

____